S0-AZU-740

"There Once Was A Woman Named Jo,

and a man who couldn't let go.'' His arms loosened fractionally, but his eyes held her fast with their laughter.

Jo reluctantly began to extricate herself. "This is embarrassing. I've never done anything like this before, Clayton," she said in a barely audible voice.

"Completed a limerick, you mean?"

"Oh, I do that all the time. Sometimes I even rewrite one of yours."

"Then what haven't you done, Joelle? Kissed a man?"

"Not in ages and ages." When the words sank in her eyes widened. "But I'm not kissing you," she protested just as his lips brushed the top of her nose. The last of her reason melted, and she became aware of the crash of thunder, the pounding of the storm-driven surf.

Was it her own heart? His?

Dear Reader,

Welcome to Silhouette! Our goal is to give you hours of unbeatable reading pleasure, and we hope you'll enjoy each month's six new Silhouette Desires. These sensual, provocative love stories are both believable and compelling—sometimes they're poignant, sometimes humorous, but always enjoyable.

Indulge yourself. Experience all the passion and excitement of falling in love along with our heroine as she meets the irresistible man of her dreams and together they overcome all obstacles in the path to a happy ending.

If this is your first Desire, I hope it'll be the first of many. If you're already a Silhouette Desire reader, thanks for your support! Look for some of your favorite authors in the coming months: Stephanie James, Diana Palmer, Dixie Browning, Ann Major and Doreen Owens Malek, to name just a few.

Happy reading!

Isabel Swift
Senior Editor

SDRL-7/85

DIXIE BROWNING
There Once Was a Lover

Silhouette Desire

Published by Silhouette Books New York

America's Publisher of Contemporary Romance

To Nora Roberts and Ruth Langan,
for making the journeys more fun
and the "elises" more endurable.

SILHOUETTE BOOKS
300 East 42nd St., New York, N.Y. 10017

Copyright © 1987 by Dixie Browning

All rights reserved, including the right to reproduce
this book or portions thereof in any form whatsoever.
For information address Silhouette Books,
300 East 42nd St., New York, N.Y. 10017

ISBN: 0-373-05337-1

First Silhouette Books printing March 1987

All the characters in this book are fictitious. Any
resemblance to actual persons, living or dead, is
purely coincidental.

SILHOUETTE, SILHOUETTE DESIRE and colophon
are registered trademarks of the publisher.

America's Publisher of Contemporary Romance

Printed in the U.S.A.

Books by Dixie Browning

Silhouette Special Editon

Finders Keepers #50
Reach Out to Cherish #110
Just Deserts #181
Time and Tide #205
By Any Other Name #228
The Security Man #314

Silhouette Desire

Shadow of Yesterday #68
Image of Love #91
The Hawk and the Honey #111
Late Rising Moon #121
Stormwatch #169
The Tender Barbarian #188
Matchmaker's Moon #212
A Bird in Hand #234
In the Palm of Her Hand #264
A Winter Woman #324
There Once Was a Lover #337

Silhouette Romance

Unreasonable Summer #12
Tumbled Wall #38
Chance Tomorrow #53
Wren of Paradise #73
East of Today #93
Winter Blossom #113
Renegade Player #142
Island on the Hill #164
Logic of the Heart #172
Loving Rescue #191
A Secret Valentine #203
Practical Dreamer #221
Visible Heart #275
Journey to Quiet Waters #292
The Love Thing #305
First Things Last #323
Something for Herself #381
Reluctant Dreamer #460

DIXIE BROWNING,

one of Silhouette's most prolific and popular authors, has written over thirty books since *Unreasonable Summer*, a Silhouette Romance, came out in 1980. She has also published books for the Desire and Special Edition lines. She is a charter member of the Romance Writers of America, and her Romance *Renegade Player* won the Golden Medallion in 1983. A charismatic lecturer, Dixie has toured extensively for Silhouette Books, participating in ''How To Write A Romance'' workshops all over the country.

Dixie's family has lived along the North Carolina coast for many generations, and it is there that she finds a great deal of inspiration. Along with her writing awards, Dixie has been acclaimed as a watercolor painter, being the first president of the Watercolor Society of North Carolina. She is also currently president of Browning Artworks, Ltd., a gallery featuring fine crafts on Hatteras Island. Although Dixie enjoys her traveling, she is always happy to return to North Carolina, where she and her husband make their home.

One

They've got to be violating *something*!" Harriet Brower declared. "All of those people living under one roof—and don't tell me they're all just visiting relatives!" She continued to pace the cluttered office, her footsteps ringing with militant authority on the bare parquet floor.

"Yes, Miss Brower," Joelle murmured.

"Hmmm... Check with Joe Brady down at city hall about the zoning."

"For the whole block, or just the Voegler house?"

Harriet glared, tugged at the foundation garment that constrained her ample girth, then snorted. "Why on earth should I be interested in a row of slums and a few acres of weeds? The Voegler house, you ninny! See when it was inspected last and what the results were."

"Will Mr. Brady give out that kind of information?"

"He will if he wants his mother-in-law to get elected to the city council. Tell him Harriet Brower sent you."

Not a flicker of the distaste she felt registered on Joelle's face as she continued to fold and stuff the letters urging the defeat of a proposed bond referendum. Two more boxes of envelopes and she'd be finished.

"Tomorrow's Saturday. If you hurry you can make it to city hall before five. Take those things with you, and don't forget the mailing list. They'll have to be hand addressed, but you can do that at home."

For a moment, Joelle continued to stuff automatically, her mind busily composing another limerick in honor of her employer.

> There once was a lady named Brower
> Who loved to—no, who gloried in wielding her power
> A registered witch, a legitimate—

"Well? *Well?* What are you waiting for?"

Reluctantly, Joelle stood, the unfinished verse forgotten. When it came to the first three lines, she was a whiz; she knew at least a dozen rhymes for both Harriet and Brower. It was the last line that usually did her in. Which was one more reason why she was in awe of Clayton Abbott, editor of the *Greensport Daily News*. Using limerick form, he zapped his targets so skillfully that they seldom even knew they'd been wounded.

"Yes, Miss Brower," she said for the hundredth time that day as she began gathering up the work to take home. There was a movie on cable she'd wanted to see, but if she stuffed envelopes while she watched, she'd end up with paper cuts. Her fingers were in bad enough shape without that.

"No, Chip—not the editorial page!" Joelle screeched the following afternoon. "If you've got to shoot baskets with today's paper, use the funnies."

"Hey! No sweat, sis." Chip shrugged his jersey-clad shoulders and began smoothing out the center section of the *Greensport Daily News*. He'd been restricted to crumpled newspaper since he'd missed the wastebasket with a real ball and knocked a vase off a shelf, dousing Ivan's cage and scattering broken glass over half the living room. "Hey, what's the matter, won't that carnivorous bird of yours do his business on the funnies?"

Ignoring the question as she did the wads of crumpled newspaper that littered her floor, Joelle tucked the editorial section into her desk drawer, moistened another envelope on the sponge and slammed her fist down on it. Harriet Brower could have afforded self-sealing envelopes; the woman owned half of Greensport.

"Aw *ri-i-ight*, way to *go*!" Chip, looking several years younger than his forty-one, lunged forward as his team scored another point, and Jo did her best go ignore the blaring TV, the potato chip crumbs and empty beer cans, plus all the other reasons why Chip was here in her living room watching the game instead of at home in his own neat-as-a-pin den. Chip's wife, Candy, wouldn't tolerate the noise and the clutter.

"Another Saturday shot to blue blazes," Jo muttered under the roar of the television crowd. Sighing, she lifted a thumbnail to her teeth and nibbled. It tasted of glue. Darn it, she'd had her weekend all planned. She'd picked up the latest Robert Ludlum from the library and bought Ivan and herself a pound of white grapes and a jar of salted cashews. She'd been all set to sleep until noon today and indulge herself shamefully until Monday morning rolled around again.

So what had happened? She been roused out of a marvelous dream at seven-twenty when Harriet had called to find out what she'd learned from Joe Brady at City Hall. Harriet was hot on the trail of her latest worthy cause, determined to broaden Greensport's tax base and double the employment possibilities by making way for a new shopping mall. Her current burst of civic-mindedness would last about as long as most of her enthusiasms did. Then another cause would come along, and the first would be forgotten as she redeployed her troops on still another front.

Unfortunately, kindness to secretaries didn't fall under the heading of worthy causes, not even for the short term. But the pay was adequate, and even more important, Jo's work kept her well in the background, for the most part. Harriet didn't care to share the limelight, and that suited Jo just fine.

Chip had shown up on her doorstep half an hour before game time, and Jo had accepted his appearance with resignation. It wasn't that she didn't love her brothers and sisters. Or her nieces and nephews and even her brothers- and sisters-in-law. But there were times when she wondered if she was anything more than a convenience to them.

"Oh, swell," she grumbled, gathering up three beer cans, a liter-sized cola bottle, and her cashew jar—all empty. "Go ahead, why not wallow in a little self-pity, you redheaded wimp? If you don't like it, stand up on your hind legs and *do* something about it!"

Ivan whistled a shrill note of commiseration, and Jo rescued half a cashew from under the sofa, dusted it off and placed it between her teeth. She opened the cage door and leaned forward until Ivan, with gracious precision, removed the nut with his scarlet bill.

"You're welcome, pretty boy. One of these days," she vowed as she went about collecting the wads of newspaper that had missed the basket, "we're going to pull the plug on our TV, padlock our apartment, take a cruise to some exotic South Sea Island and stay gone until basketball and baseball and football seasons are over!"

The lovebird climbed to the top of his cage and swaggered back and forth bobbing his head in agreement.

"One of these days I'm going to open your door while Chip or Hal are slam-dunking wastepaper all over my living room, and let nature take its course."

Ivan detested men. Joelle was inclined to share his views, but usually by the time she'd finished picking up after a game, her temper had fizzled out. Griping helped, and Ivan was a discreet and sympathetic confidant.

"One of these days," she promised in a burst of generosity, "I'm going to find you a mate, mate."

One of these days, she'd like to think she'd find one for herself, but Joelle was a realist. Her chances, never great, grew slimmer with each passing year.

After dinner, *à deux*—peanut butter and cucumber sandwich for her, a string bean and a few sunflower seeds for Ivan—Jo withdrew the crumpled editorial page from the desk drawer, switched on a reading light, and curled up on the sofa. The self-indulgent weekend she'd planned was out—she wasn't in the mood for Ludlum—but at least she'd managed to salvage one treat.

"The man is not only brilliant, Ive, he's sensitive, witty, and courageous." She read through the house editorial, and then started at the top and read more slowly, examining the thought processes that had led to Clayton Abbott's conclusions. She'd never even seen his picture, much less met him face to face, but in the two years since he'd become editor of Greensport's daily newspaper, he had revealed himself to be everything she'd ever longed for in a man. Realist or not, Jo had begun to allow herself the occasional fantasy.

"Well, what's so crazy about that?" she demanded of the bird who strolled across her shoulders, grooming Joelle's wild crop of red curls. "You look at a picture of a female Fischer and start preening. Millions of women palpitate over pictures of Elvis or Valentino. It just so happens that I get turned on by the way a man's mind works. Is that so weird?''

Fantasizing, Jo told herself, was a perfectly harmless pastime as long as one's feet were planted firmly on the ground. As for being infatuated with a man she'd never even met, it happened all the time. It might be slightly juvenile, but it was harmless enough. Actually, exploring the workings of a man's mind was much more intimate than merely exploring the arrangement of his features.

Ivan grew more demanding, and Jo stroked the top of his tiny head with a forefinger. "Don't be jealous, lovie. It's not as if I'm in any danger of going off the deep end. I simply need a little more mental stimulation than you can provide. You're adorable, sport, but you're no mental giant.''

She read the other editorials, and then reread Clayton Abbott's. Tonight's piece was far more personal than usual, and Jo felt a thrill that was almost physical as she thought about the man as a boy. He had touched on a volatile situation that had arisen with the local board of education, and then gone on to write about the teacher who had suspended him from his eighth grade English class some twenty years ago. She had been thoroughly despised at the time for her unrelenting insistence on learning. The value of her methods and the extent of her sacrifices on behalf of her students had become evident only later.

"Miss Carruthers," Jo murmured, remembering her sixth grade English teacher, loved by none, feared by all. Miss Carruthers had conducted her classes the way General Patton had conducted his troops. It was thanks to Miss Carruthers that Jo, with only a high school diploma and a short business course, was able to rise to Harriet Brower's demanding standards.

"You certainly don't dress like a lady," Harriet had said in the course of their interview, "but at least you speak like one. You know the difference between a noun and a verb, and you can spell. That's more than I can say for a single one of the other applicants."

Jo smiled now at the modest by-line. "Who but you, darling Clay, would take the time to publicly thank a school teacher who once suspended you from English class?" she murmured. Another meeting of the minds. It took a strong man to voluntarily admit to having made a fool of himself, even twenty years before.

Twenty years ago he'd been in the eight grade. That would make him... not nearly as old as Jo had imagined.

On Tuesday Harriet asked her to drive them to the old Voegler house. Joelle loved driving Harriet's yacht-sized sedan—the chariot, she called it in her modest attempts at composing limericks. If there were going to be fireworks, however, she'd just as soon forego the pleasure.

"Park across the street," Harriet ordered.

"But the sign says No Parking."

"As long as there's someone in the car, it's not parked," Harriet retorted with a prime example of her own convoluted logic. "I'll wait here while you copy down all the names of the tenants. There ought to be a list in the lobby."

Jo cringed. "But Miss Brower—"

"Would you look at that! That woman's seventy if she's a day, and she's looking after three children under school age. Make a note! We'll just see if anyone in that old fire-trap is licensed as a day-care operator. Go on, go on—what are you waiting for? I don't have all day!"

Jo clamped her lips shut and dug out her notebook. Some days were more difficult than others, and this was one of them. She scribbled herself a note and toyed briefly with the idea of adding her resignation, tossing it into Harriet's face and running.

She lacked the guts. Aside from the fact that she could spell, the main reason she'd lasted as long as she had was a constitutional inability to make waves.

Harriet liked her minions to be silent, obedient, and strong as horses. Thanks to a mixture of genes and conditioning, Jo was all of the above. Being the middle sibling might have had something to do with it. None of the Middletons ever caught colds. Not one of them had ever broken a bone. Except for her, they were all outgoing, gregarious, and ambitious. They were all extremely attractive—the sort of people who never had a pimple in their lives, who always had perfect checkups. Except for her. Jo had had two cavities before she'd even got her permanent teeth.

On the rare occasions when Jo thought about her appearance these days, it was with a sense of amused resignation. Surely she was supposed to have been another typical Middleton, collecting her share of medals and trophies as she breezed through college on a scholarship. Like Chip, Fran, Sybil, and Hal, she'd been genetically programmed to zoom to success in her chosen career, and one day marry a successful, handsome man and produce a pair of precocious, photogenic babies who never even drooled.

Only someone had screwed up. Badly. Jo detested sports. If you didn't count that horrid sales rep that Fran's husband, Pete, had fixed her up with, she hadn't had a real date in over a year, and any cleverness to which she could lay claim invariably came in the middle of the night, when it didn't count. Oh, she was great at composing scathingly brilliant, witty dialogue when she was all alone, but in the company of another person, her lips were sealed, her tongue froze and her brain congealed. She was about as witty as your typical pillar of salt.

Clay Abbott continued to concentrate his efforts on the city's few remaining historical gems, using as his prime example the old Voegler place. The multi-turreted frame house had been built at a time when Greensport's future had glittered with promise. The decline of the railroad had put an end to that. One by one, the small industries had withered and died, or else moved to more promising areas, and Greensport had drifted into a gentle depression. Except for a few families whose wealth remained secure—the Browers, the Humphlettes, the Treagers—people began moving to more promising areas. At least the younger ones did. For the older ones, relocating was out of the question. They simply hung on and endured.

Now, thanks to a new link of interstate highway, Greensport was beginning to experience a renaissance. As new industries began to look about for cheap land and available labor, towns like Greensport began to sit up and rub the sleep from their eyes. Shabby business districts were quickly refurbished in the hope of attracting both customers and new venture capital. In the rush, many of the old white elephants were cleared away to make room for office buildings and new apartment complexes.

Now there were too few white elephants left. As Clay reminded his readers, white elephants were an endangered species. Like the passenger pigeons or the Carolina parakeet, once gone, they could never be recalled. The Voegler house was a valuable piece of history, sagging balconies, broken millwork and peeling brown paint notwithstanding. He wrote:

Only three of these wonderful old mansions survive. Destroy those and you've destroyed an important part of your heritage. The role of every building is twofold, its influence felt both by those who use it and those who see it from the outside. Before we destroy the old to make way for the new, we must ask ourselves whether our lives will be the richer for the change.

Harriet was livid. "Who does he think he is? A rank outsider, a carpetbagging, meddlesome— What right does he have to come here and . . ."

Joelle buried her head in the draft of a flyer she was editing and tried to ignore the tirade. She'd have thought Harriet would have applauded the sentiments. After all, the Browers had been here since the War Between the States. The Middletons hadn't arrived until several generations later.

It was even worse the following day. There'd been a limerick in the morning paper. Jo could put away a straight editorial, savoring the coming delight all day long, but the limericks were irresistible, and it was impossible not to peek.

> A lady was once so annoyed
> That she ordered a castle destroyed.
> Said she, it's a pity,
> But that part of the city
> Would be much more valuable void.

"Take a letter, Joella!" In high dudgeon, Harriet always added a syllable to Jo's name, as if she needed more to sink her teeth into than a name that rhymed with Noel.

Jo cringed at the tone of the letter. Charges, threats, and demands. Perhaps she'd forget to append her initials. In the rare event that they ever met, she'd hate to have Clayton Abbott think she'd been a party to any of this.

"I'll get it out today, Miss Brower," she said meekly, reeling a sheet of stationery into her machine.

"You'll deliver it by hand."

"I can get it to the post office in time to—"

"If you value your overpaid position, Missy, you'll do as I say. I want you to deliver that letter directly to Clayton Abbott. Not to his secretary, either. I want it delivered into his hands, and I want you to stand there and see that he reads it, is that clear?"

Jo's teeth clicked against her fingertips as she frantically searched for a shred of nail long enough to nibble.

"Stop that disgusting habit this minute! You're old enough to know better. Now finish it, and I'll sign it and then you can go for the day, but call me as soon as you get home and let me know what happened, do you understand?"

I'll resign on the spot, Jo vowed silently. I'll drop the letter in the nearest mail box and then go visit Aunt Lanie in Columbia until it all blows over. Or maybe I'll join the Navy and see the world.

"Well? *Well?* Write, girl, write! Or have you finally chewed your fingers off?"

Shoulders heaving in a sigh, Jo bent over her task. Maybe Clayton Abbott's secretary would snatch the letter from her hands, in which case, Harriet could hardly blame Jo for not carrying out her demands.

She was not to be so fortunate. According to the receptionist at the newspaper office, both Mr. Abbott and his secretary had gone for the day. The woman offered to give him the letter when he came in the following morning, and Jo hesitated. Integrity struggled with cowardice, and integrity won.

"Oh, I was instructed specifically to hand-deliver this. I'd better drop it by his home," she said reluctantly.

The receptionist reached for a lipstick-stained coffee mug that bore a suggestive slogan. "Suit yourself, hon."

"Do you happen to have his address?" Jo half expected the woman to refuse to reveal it. No such luck.

"You know the old MacLuckie Farm Road? Take that for about three miles, then take the first dirt road to the right. Can't miss it. Circle around a pond and keep going until you come to the house."

This was too much. If he'd been in his office and she could have simply handed over the letter and left, that would have been one thing, but to have to drive five miles out of her way, when it was already getting dark...

It wasn't that she was afraid of the man, Jo told herself earnestly as she left the building and headed for her car. She might not be as gregarious as the rest of her family—all right, she was a little bit shy. But that wasn't the only factor in this particular instance.

The truth was, Jo had really enjoyed her harmless fantasies. After today they'd no longer be possible. It was one thing to fantasize about the intimate workings of a man's mind when she hadn't the foggiest idea what he looked like. He was probably dour-faced, with stringy hair and nicotine-stained fingers. He probably wore a battered old felt hat and had egg stains on his tie.

"Talk about exploding myths," she muttered. It was a darned shame, too. She was at her scintillating best mentally debating the finer points of his editorials and trying to match him limerick for limerick.

Extricating her compact car from a tight parking slot, she turned in the opposite direction from her apartment, determined that this would be the last stop. If he didn't answer the doorbell, she'd shove the blasted thing under his door and leave. And if by chance her hero answered the door in person, she'd close her eyes before she saw too much.

What if his eyes were closed, too? Jo had never harbored any illusions about her own attractions. She was too tall, too thin, her hair was the color of iron rust and unless she kept it tightly braided, it looked like unraveled rope. Her neck was too long and so was her nose, her ears stood out like little pink wings, and she had the sort of freckles that never quite faded, even in the dead of winter.

"We make a great pair," she mused several minutes later as she pulled up in front of a rambling structure of rock, glass and rough wood siding. "They say like attracts like. A ten rates a ten, and a two rates a two." Maybe his wife would answer the door. At this point, it hardly mattered.

Clay hung up his coat in the closet and then remembered his necktie. He'd do better to leave a selection of ties in his office in case he needed one instead of wearing them half a day and then stuffing them into his coat pocket.

God, he was beat! It wasn't enough that he'd been operating shorthanded for months, now half his staff was down with the flu, and he was just beginning to find out that the Brower woman carried a bigger stick than he'd thought. She didn't walk all that softly, either. Two of his biggest advertisers had called this morning, wondering if he wasn't placing too much emphasis on saving a worn-out old firetrap that should have been razed years ago. It hadn't taken much imagination to see Harriet's fine hand in all this.

When the doorbell sounded, he swore softly and put the bottle back on the bar. One undisturbed drink in the peace of his own home, was that too much to ask? He was tempted to ignore the bell, but it might be something important. Some worthy subscriber wanting him to do a Sunday feature about her little darling's first piano recital. Wouldn't be the first time he'd been tracked to his lair by a determined hunter.

Flinging open the door, Clay glared at the intruder on his doorstep. At first he took her to be a high school kid. The freckles and braid, the baggy jeans, the pinched look—as if she were afraid he'd bite her head off.

"Mr. Abbott?" Her voice was somewhere between a croak and a whisper.

"What is it, cookies or magazine subscriptions?"

"No sir, I—my employer—I—this—" Jo closed her eyes, her fingers tightening on the letter she clutched in one hand.

"Come in, come in, but make it quick, will you?"

When he stepped away from the door, Jo didn't know what else to do. She didn't want to go inside his house. She wanted to hand the letter over and run, but how could she when he kept moving away from her?

This was Clayton Abbott? *This* was her hero? But this was *awful*!

"Dammit, are you coming inside, or not? I hate to shut the door in your face, but I don't intend to stand here until the whole county's had the benefit of my furnace."

In a state resembling shock, Jo lurched through the open door, came to a halt a foot away from the tall, dangerously attractive man, and froze. She'd never been more self-conscious in her life as she felt his eyes moving over her, missing nothing—not a single detail, from her scruffy sneakers to the last freckle on her naked face. Why, oh why had she held out against Harriet, against her own sisters, when it came to the matter of clothes? What harm would it have done to wear an occasional dress? Just because she felt like a scarecrow in drag when she tried on the things Fran and Sybil picked out for her—just because she had legs like stilts and no more bosom at twenty-seven than she'd had at fourteen—that didn't mean she had to wear baggy pants and shapeless tops for the rest of her natural life.

"Well?"

The single word, spoken in a gravelly baritone, had the effect of paralyzing her still further. *I'm dying. My feet are already numb. Someone take care of Ivan for me, please.*

Helplessly, Jo continued to stare up into the most magnificent face she'd ever seen on any man. Eyes the same rich blue as an October sky. Oh, yes, she'd spotted the intelligence in them right away, if none of the warmth and humor she'd imagined. In a rugged, tanned face, under a thick crop of dark-brown hair, they were his most striking feature.

In spite of his impatience, Clay felt a tug of amusement. The woman looked as if she were frightened stiff. And she was a woman, not a child, as he'd first thought. "I seldom bite, you know," he said in an effort to break the stalemate. "That's only a nasty rumor."

"M-my employer—that is, there's this letter—"

Clay's eyes fell to the envelope she was clutching in her fist. He waited. With no idea who her employer was, he could hardly guess the contents of the letter, but he could stand here as long as it took. This was becoming mildly interesting, as tired as he was.

Actually, Clay admitted to himself, she was the sort of woman nine people out of ten would look right past without even seeing. The tenth would be well rewarded for his efforts. There was something about her...

As she seemed in no hurry to hand over the letter, he took the time to examine her more thoroughly. Flawless bone structure. Not really pretty, but with the sort of beauty that never really faded. Her eyes, he decided with the deliberation of a connoisseur, were probably her most striking feature. Nothing subtle about those; they were enormous, the soft gray-green of a certain type of jade, but clear as a mountain stream. Probably slightly nearsighted, as well, he noted.

As for her hair, it was hard to tell. Fiery red and all but impossible to tame, he suspected, it had been pulled back into a merciless style that would have been disastrous on anyone with less than her perfect bone structure. It lent her the austere look of a prima ballerina. The nose? Elegant rather than cute. The mouth, wide—possibly given to laughter when she wasn't stricken with whatever ailed her at the moment.

As for the rest of her, Clay summed up, stepping back for a better view, it was hard to tell under all those layers. The tattered look. Was that still 'In'? It took so long for fashions to filter down to this sleepy little mini-metropolis he lost track. Not that he'd ever been overly concerned beyond the demands of his work.

It occurred to him that this woman would have made a hell of a fashion model, but somehow he couldn't see her exhibiting herself, either on a runway or for the impersonal eye of a camera.

"Who are you?" he inquired softly, halfway intrigued in spite of himself.

"This is for you." Jo finally managed to get out. She rammed the rumpled letter toward him and would have bolted, but Clay was faster than she was.

He caught her by the wrist and held her there. "Wait a minute, you haven't answered my question. Who are you? What are you doing here? And is this thing going to explode in my face if I open it?"

Two

So Dirty Harry wants me to back off, does she?" Clay said softly after scanning the letter Jo had typed.

She swallowed, her eyes moving around the magnificent rooms in view of the front door. Her own cramped apartment would have fitted nicely into just the space she could see from here. "I'd better be going," she murmured, edging away reluctantly. Now that she was actually here, she found herself in danger of taking root.

"What do you think, should I let up on her? I haven't even started to turn up the heat yet, but if Lady Harriet insists..."

Here's your chance, you ninny! Clayton Abbott was actually asking her opinion. She'd been brilliant enough in her response with only Ivan as an audience; what was stopping her now?

"Come on, I'm interested. You're a citizen of Greensport as well as a friend of Harriet Brower."

"I'm only her secretary," Jo corrected. "We're hardly friends." Then, feeling disloyal, she hurried to amend the statement. "Actually, I admire her enormously, even if we're not exactly—uh . . ."

"Of course you do," Clay said gravely. "She's . . . quite a woman. Do you agree that we should allow one of our last remaining historical treasures to be demolished to make way for another commercial strip? Even discounting the fact that the thirty-seven people who live there will be displaced."

"Oh, I—mmm, well..." *That's right, bowl him over with those snappy comebacks, Jo.*

"Look, would you like a drink or something? I was just about to pour myself one when you arrived. We can discuss the matter in a little more comfort."

"Oh, no, please, I can't stay."

"But I haven't decided how to reply to this letter yet."

Ignoring her weak suggestions that he mail his reply, Clay stepped farther into the foyer, and not knowing how to extricate herself, Jo followed. Her bones had turned to Styrofoam, her muscles to quivering jelly, and as to what was happening to her mind, she didn't even want to know.

"Sure you don't want a drink? No? But I could still do with an unbiased opinion." Shifting his weight to the other foot, Clay stroked the late-day stubble that roughened his jaw. Why the hell had he invited her inside? He was bushed. He needed a drink, a shower, a shave and something to eat. He had his birds to see to, reams of reading to do, and a column to write. So now he found himself entertaining some big-eyed waif who'd turned up on his doorstep—and the screwy part was that he was beginning to enjoy it.

Jo opened her mouth, but no sound came forth. Pretend he's your brother, she told herself helpfully. She'd never found herself at a loss for words where her immediate family was concerned. She was simply too outnumbered to voice them, as a rule.

Cutting him a quick sidelong glance, she sighed. Pretend Clayton Abbott was her brother? Fat chance.

"The Voegler place, what do you think? Is it worth saving?"

"Well, I—I've never actually been inside. I'm not even sure it's safe. All those rickety balconies..."

"Tell Harriet to send over a crew of carpenters. The place could probably use it, although she should caution them against any real structural changes."

"That's the landlord's job. The owner should be the one to see about maintenance."

"Exactly."

"You're not implying—?"

"Yep. Precisely what you're inferring. Try not to overdo the look of surprise."

"But the Voegler house is owned by a conglomerate," Jo protested, missing the implied insult.

Clay let it pass. For the moment. "All right, forget sagging balconies. We're not talking about Romeo and Juliet here, we're talking about a group of retired people, most of whom have lived there since the place was turned into a boarding house. They're old enough to avoid rotten balconies and leaning turrets."

It occurred to Jo that the outward signs of decay might not be the most treacherous, but she hadn't come to get personally involved in the matter.

"By now," Clayton went on, "they're more like one family than nine individual couples. Some of the couples might not even be couples, for that matter."

At her questioning look, he smiled. "I only meant there might not be a framed marriage license hanging over every bed. Does that bother you?"

Jo shook her head vigorously as his meaning became clear. "Goodness, no," she exclaimed, and he laughed aloud.

The conversation had led them from the foyer to the other side of a massive rock wall. Jo found herself in a sunken square before an immense fireplace. There was a small Oriental rug on the flagstone floor, and a deep, leather-covered sofa had been built-in around two sides of the enclosure.

Clay gestured her to a seat. "So what do you think—history should give way to progress? Man's commerce takes precedence over man's castle?" He began to pace, and Jo found herself at eye level with a most fascinating part of his anatomy.

"Mmm—well, I—uh..." *He* had a better figure than *she* did, she thought with dismay. Those narrow, muscular hips, the firm, taut buttocks. As skinny as she was, her hip bones flared out, with very little padding except in the rear.

"If your lady boss needs a worthy cause, why not launch a campaign to raise funds for the restoration of Voegler House?" Clay continued. "It worked for the old Treager place. Since it was restored and turned into an arts and crafts center, it comes closer each year to being self-supporting."

"But what would happen to the residents? They'd live in a museum or another arts center?"

"There'd be plenty of time during the fund-raising stages to come up with alternate housing. The trouble is, thanks to a quirk of Greensport's outdated property laws, if the property changes hands, they can be legally evicted with practically no notice."

"Which is it you're really interested in, Mr. Abbott?" Jo asked. "The residents or the house?"

"Both. If Harriet has her way, the whole works will be scrapped. The people out on the sidewalks to fend for themselves, the house demolished. All I'm asking for is a little forethought. Why should all of Greensport be the poorer for one woman's greed?"

"*Greed?* You can't mean Harriet," Jo protested. "Miss Brower is the most generous woman I've ever known." Well, she amended silently, if not with money, at least with her time and efforts. "Her whole life is devoted to worthy causes. I should know, I've worked for her for years."

"Lady Brower wants her bread buttered on both sides, and she doesn't care where the butter comes from. Regardless of who actually holds the deed, Voegler House belongs to the community. Harriet has a responsibility—"

"I keep telling you, it has nothing to *do* with Harriet! She doesn't own the place, some out-of-state conglomerate does. She told me so, and Harriet Brower wouldn't lie," Jo said flatly.

Clay suddenly found himself captured by those deep gray-green eyes. Could anyone in this day and age be as naive, as idealistic as she seemed to be?

He planted himself in front of her, feet spread apart, hands on his hips. His rumpled white shirt was open at the throat, the sleeves rolled back to reveal muscular, hair-covered forearms. "Then why is she so anxious to have the place brought down?" he demanded softly.

"To make way for the new shopping center."

"Does Greensport really need another shopping center? The one we have is barely making a go of it. Competition from a new kid on the block isn't going to help."

"But the jobs—"

"The jobs lost when the old shops go under?"

Jo bit her lip and managed to tear her eyes away from his belt buckle. "I still think you're wrong," she whispered. "These things aren't—the backers wouldn't—I'm sure..." She was sure of nothing anymore, except that her life would never be quite the same after having been exposed to Clayton Abbott in the flesh.

"The backers wouldn't go into this thing blind, is that what you were going to say?"

Wordlessly, she nodded.

"Hmmm, maybe. You've given me a new slant, though. I've been so preoccupied with keeping the wreckers from doing away with an architectural gem, I overlooked that point." A blue flame danced in his eyes, lighting the way for his quick, warm smile. "You've been a big help, uh—say, what is your name, anyway?"

Jo felt the embarrassing rush of heat on her throat, and then her face. The curse of the thin-skinned redhead. Unfortunately, short of pulling her coat collar up over her face, there was no way of hiding. Dammit, why hadn't she inherited the whole redheaded bag of tricks? If she had any gumption, she wouldn't even be here. She'd have told Harriet to deliver her own letter!

With growing understanding, Clay watched the flush of color rise and fall, leaving hundreds of freckles standing out in clear relief. Blushing? A grown woman? Neither of them had said anything that could possibly be construed as embarrassing. Surely she wasn't...

Shy? Good God, he'd thought the species extinct by now.

Kneeling before her, he said, "Please forgive me if I've embarrassed you in any way. It was purely unintentional, I assure you. I'm Clayton Abbott."

"Of course you are," Jo said gruffly, forcing herself to react like a normal adult instead of an adolescent fruitcake.

"And you are? I'm afraid I completely forgot my manners."

Jo melted. "Joelle Middleton," she whispered, sinking still further under his spell. The man was a direct descendant of Merlin.

"I'm delighted to meet you, Joelle Middleton."

"I've been a—a fan of yours for ages, Mr. Abbott," she confessed, determined not to waste this opportunity. She'd probably never get another one. "Your limericks, especially. I just wanted to...thank you."

"You're welcome," Clayton replied gravely. "Does being a fan mean you agree with my editorial opinions?"

Jo might occasionally indulge in a face-saving daydream, but when it came to her dealings with other people, she was scrupulously honest. "No. Usually I do, but not always."

"You've never written a letter to the editor expressing your disagreement?"

"I write one once in a while, but I'd never send them. No anonymous letters—it says so at the bottom of the column," Jo reminded him with the merest shadow of a smile. "I'd never have the nerve to go public with an opinion."

"Pity. I have an idea your opinion would be well worth discovering." Before Jo could recover from that, he said thoughtfully, "Joelle. That's an unusual name. Your father must be named Joel, right?"

Jo was beginning to feel remarkably at ease, considering the circumstances. She felt the smile tug a little more strongly at the corners of her mouth. "My father's name was Herbert. I was named for a great uncle. We were named for relatives—all five of us."

"Hmm, strong family ties. Must be nice. I was the only child of an only child."

"That's sad." The smile gave way to a look of commiseration. "I'm not sure it was all sentiment, though—our names, I mean. Just before I was born, Uncle Joel made a killing in hog futures, and I think my parents hoped I'd be remembered in his will.''

Clay watched the subtle changes of expression come and go on her mobile face. God, the woman was exquisite! It was like discovering a priceless *objet d'art* in a dusty junk shop. "Go on, I'm interested. The inner workings of large families have always fascinated me.''

Jo shrugged, finally giving way to the smile that had been threatening to appear ever since he'd knelt in front of her. "Anyway, Uncle Joel doubled his fortune by investing it in wheat futures, and after that he bought a share of a race horse. He even came out ahead in that deal, but then he lost the whole bundle in pork bellies. That sounds pretty disgusting, but Daddy explained that it was actually boxcar loads of pork—but you'd know that, of course.''

Clay nodded, not wanting to interrupt the flow. She had an unusual voice—deep, soft, slightly husky. It was remarkably soothing after the chaotic atmosphere of the newspaper office.

"Uncle Joel was an all-or-nothing sort of man, you might say. If he believed in something, he went all the way.''

"Evidently he believed in bacon.''

Jo nodded as her eyes explored the texture of his thick, mahogany-colored hair. "Poor Uncle Joel. He always blamed the surgeon general for ruining his health and welfare. There was a big antifat and cholesterol campaign just about the time he staked everything he owned on pigs.''

"The vagaries of the commodities market,'' Clay mused. "Say, would you like that drink I promised you? Or maybe something to eat? My housekeeper leaves something reheatable in the refrigerator three days a week.''

"Oh, no, I'd better go.'' Jo tore her eyes away from his hypnotic gaze to stare at the floor. She rammed her fists deeper into the pockets of the coat she'd never bothered to remove and looked at her scruffy sneakers on what was probably a priceless Oriental rug. She finally got to meet her hero face to face, and she looked like something the cat had left on the doorstep.

"We're just beginning to get acquainted. Do you really have to go?"

Miserably, Jo nodded. She really did. For just a minute there, she'd sounded almost coherent—better leave while she was ahead.

"Perhaps another time, then. May I call you?"

Alarmed, she shook her head. "I—I work," she blurted.

"All the time?"

Again she nodded, her braid flopping its way into her collar. "Miss Brower doesn't keep regular hours. Sometimes I—I never know—"

With a look of gentle amusement, Clay reached out and removed her hair from the collar of her padded jacket. When he took her left hand in his, Jo could have died. At least they were clean—she'd scrubbed them furiously after changing the ribbon in her machine that morning, but her nails...

Harriet was right. It was a disgustingly childish habit. She'd never *ever* do it again, she vowed.

There was no letup. As a rule, Clay did no more than three editorials a week, but something told Jo that he wasn't about to let Harriet off the hook on this one.

She was right. No limerick, but instead, a thoughtful survey of Greensport's limited housing alternatives. "Meeting the needs of a diverse population is never an easy task," Clay had written. "At times it becomes impossible to serve one group without imposing hardship on another."

"Is he talking about the two different shopping centers?" Jo demanded of her usual sounding board, Ivan. She read on. "Our needs, our desires, our very values differ. At what point does the common welfare take precedence over the individual's?"

She considered that statement. Her own needs were fairly simple—a roof over her head, enough money for food, clothing, and birdseed, and a bit extra to throw away on such frivolous things as health insurance and car payments. As for her desires, those had undergone a rather startling metamorphosis in the past few days.

"It is imperative that we move quickly where the people's welfare is concerned; equally imperative that we do not, in our haste, destroy that which cannot be replaced."

"All right, you blue-eyed wonder, I'll give you an A-plus for that one, but what about—" She tried hard to come up with a legitimate argument, and finding none, sighed. "I wish you could have met him, Ivan."

Ivan canted a beady eye in her direction, and Jo decided that it was just as well they hadn't met. Ivan was extremely territorial, not to mention jealous. He considered Jo his property, and with his razor-sharp beak, he was well able to defend his claim.

The following week, a letter from Harriet Brower appeared on the editorial page. Jo didn't bother to read it. She'd not only had to type it, but she'd been forced to deliver it by hand.

"Why not mail it, Miss Brower?" she'd asked.

"What, and have them claim it had never been delivered? I didn't get to be this age without learning a thing or two, Joella."

"But what if Mr. Abbott's busy? Or tied up all day in a meeting? Your letter might not get in tomorrow's edition."

"Well...all right, in that case, give it to his secretary, but be sure you tell her who sent it. I want her to know I'll be watching for it."

There had followed a veritable duel of irate letters from Harriet and clever limericks from Clayton. In all honesty, Jo could sympathize with both viewpoints. The Voegler house was a fantastic old ruin, but it *was* a ruin, and probably far too dangerous for anyone to be living in. Maybe it was best for all concerned that they demolish it before someone was seriously hurt.

But when Clay quoted Churchill by saying that "We shape our buildings and then our buildings shape us," Jo had been compelled to admit that a large part of Greensport's personality was tied up in its huge trees and its wonderful old buildings. Without those, it could be any town in any state.

On the other hand, renovation cost money. The town already had an arts center. What would it do with another restored white elephant? And where would all the people go?

There once was a maddening man, Jo mused, *Who moved like a plague through the land. He rattled the town and shook it around, till it dwelt in the palm of his hand.*

Not bad, she judged. Not up to Abbott standards, of course, but then, who was? "Dwelt in the palm of his hand?" she repeated aloud as she set the parking brake and stared at the big, square Brower house. Joelle Middleton might snuggle up in that broad, capable palm quite happily, but she doubted that Harriet Brower ever would.

Harriet was waiting, flowered hat planted squarely on her head, elderly mink coat meeting around her ample girth. "Don't take anything off, we don't have time to waste."

It was the beginning of what were possibly the worst three days of Jo's life. They covered almost a third of the residential district the first day, knocking on every door with

Harriet's petition. Harriet was in her element; Jo was decidedly not in hers.

Clay's editorials had had their effect, and Jo cringed every time someone refused to sign. She cringed every time Harriet's booming voice rang out to demand that some stranger read and sign her petition. She cringed each time they trooped up another front walk, Harriet carrying the battle flag and Jo bringing up the rear, armed with a supply of sharpened pencils as well as the voluminous petition.

On the fourth day, Harriet gloated. "All right, let's see what that meddling carpetbagger has to say now," she pronounced smugly. "Joella, I want you to deliver this into Clayton Abbott's hands and demand that he publish this statement and every single signature in the Sunday edition."

"You mean now?" Jo cringed again. It was five-fifteen. There wasn't a chance she could catch him at the office.

"Now!"

Just as the sun sent its last feeble warmth across the wooded countryside, Jo found herself once more knocking on Clayton's front door. Shivering, she rammed her fists deeper into the pockets of her padded navy jacket. Perhaps he wasn't home. It was Friday; he probably had a date. He'd probably picked up some woman right after work, and even now they were having a drink in some cozy, intimate bar.

She shivered and rang again, finding no comfort at all in the thought of Clayton Abbott's entertaining some beauty queen with a doctorate in sheer brilliance for drinks and dinner and who knows what else.

"Hello, Joelle."

The words caught her up short. She'd already turned away, and now she looked over her shoulder, a wide smile breaking across her face. "Oh—I thought maybe you weren't here." *You're hopeless, you wimp, utterly hopeless!*

"Do you always give up so easily?"

"I rang and knocked."

"Three times. It takes me that long to get from my bedroom to the front door."

"Oh," she whispered lamely, fists threatening to punch through the lining of her pockets.

"Come on in, Joelle. I assume you've come on another mission from my worthy adversary?"

"I'm afraid so." Torn between reluctance and a wild desire to throw herself at him, Jo stepped past him into the warmth of the rock-walled foyer, her eyes studiously downcast.

Closing the massive front door, Clay watched her with growing amusement. A most extraordinary creature, he concluded. She moved with the awkward grace of a giraffe and dressed with a total disregard for style. She appeared to be almost terminally shy, and yet she worked for a steam roller like Harriet Brower. On the other hand, he'd venture a guess that Dirty Harry didn't condone the shabby corduroy jeans, the sneakers and the shapeless coat. She'd evidently gone a few rounds with that old battle ax and come out a winner, so perhaps she wasn't as spineless as she appeared.

"Better take off your coat while I see what she's dreamed up this time." Clay held out his hand, and Jo handed over the plump manila envelope that had been tucked securely under her arm. "Your coat. Let me hang it up for you."

"Oh, no, that's all right," Jo said hurriedly.

"Joelle." Clay's softly voiced rebuke had her scrambling out of it in seconds. She hadn't meant to be rude, it was just that . . .

"Had I better sit down before I open this? Looks like she's launched the heavy artillery this time."

The gentle teasing note was just what Jo needed to relax the paralyzing tension that gripped her whenever she found herself in his company. Although to be quite honest, it wasn't only Clay who affected her this way. Jo always froze up in the presence of other people. School had been agony for her, church little better. As long as she could hide behind someone larger and keep her mouth closed, she got by. It hadn't been unbearable as long as no attention was focused directly on her, but it had been no picnic. No one understood how she felt, and she'd never been able to explain. It didn't make sense, not even to her. A few of her teachers had been brutal in their efforts to cure her of shyness, and that had only made things worse.

"What am I supposed to do with this, frame it and hang it over my mantel to keep me humble?"

Jo curled her mutilated fingertips into her palms and hid them under the hem of her oversized sweater. "I think you're supposed to publish it," she said apologetically. "In Sunday's paper?" Her voice cracked on the last request, and Clay placed the letter on the table and turned to face her.

"Do you think I should?"

As he waited for her reply, he nearly forgot the question. His eyes became lost in the clear depths of hers. In danger of drowning, he managed to drag them away, only to find himself captivated by the vulnerable shadows at her temples. Gossamer skin, its ivory paleness brushed by a delightful flurry of freckles, by the fluctuating color that came and went in her cheeks and by those faint blue veins. Her breasts would be the color of skim milk, he mused. And her nipples? Would they be dark or light? Pale pink, he decided. Like the inside of a cockle shell.

"Oh, I—uh..." Jo stared at him earnestly. "Aren't you supposed to? Isn't it sort of like a public service or something?"

Clay shook his head. How old was she? Had she always been this way, or had working for the Brower woman intimidated her to the point of paranoia? "I don't have to publish anything. I'm not even sure this is in the public interest. What do you think?"

What did she think? That she wished he wouldn't sit so close to her, Jo thought wildly. That she wished she hadn't passed up her sister Fran's offer of the black faille suit and the orange gauze blouse. Not that she could see herself wearing either. "I think—hmmm, well, actually, I think I'd better be going."

"So soon? You just got here. This time, surely you'll accept my hospitality. How about coffee? Tea? Milk?"

Jo laughed. Her fists came out from under her sweater, and she brushed away a wisp of hair that had somehow escaped confinement. Tomorrow she was going to see about making an appointment with Fran's hairdresser. Surely the technology had improved since she'd had her hair cut and straightened twelve years before. It had been disastrous. She'd come out looking like an orange fake-fur pom-pom. "Coffee," she said impulsively.

"Coffee it is," Clay replied, getting to his feet. He turned, pointed a finger at her, and said, "Don't move. Be back in a minute and a half. Here—want something to read?" He snatched up a book on the history of the Hapsburg empire and plopped it into her hands. "Music? I'll put on a tape."

Again Jo's laughter rang out, and Clay backed out of the room, half afraid she'd disappear the minute he was out of sight. She was beginning to interest him. Not only his brain, but his body, which didn't make any sense at all. He was no satyr, but all the same...a woman like Joelle Middleton? In the first place, she was wacky. She was completely off the wall.

And yet, now and then he caught a glimpse of a fey creature who slipped away before he could bring her into focus.

Objectively speaking, she was a mess. Tall, a bit too thin, if she possessed an ounce of social grace, it was nowhere in evidence. Yet there was something about her, an elusive beauty that owed nothing at all to clothes or makeup.

God, those pathetic nails of hers! Once she'd gotten past her initial paralysis, he'd seen wit, intelligence and warmth peering out of those remarkable eyes, yet her nails were chewed off to the cuticles. She had the sort of ankles that could be described as aristocratic—although having seen a few royal ankles, Clay could vouch for the fact that few of them measured up to their billing. So what did she do? Hide them under bedraggled corduroy and grubby athletic shoes.

"Joelle—cream and sugar?" he called out.

"Yes, please to both."

Clay hunted up something presentable in which to pour some milk, balanced the burden on a small tray and shouldered the swinging door open. "I discovered a cold roasted chicken in the refrigerator. How would a chicken sandwich sound later?"

"I don't know. I'm not sure I've ever heard one," Jo replied, without a glimmer of a smile. Ivan appreciated her brand of humor—her family had always looked at her as if she were short a few marbles.

Clay didn't miss a beat. "Naturally, it depends on the accompaniment. My ear's not too good—if it sounds flat to you, we might want to add a slice or two of sharp cheese."

Closing her eyes, Jo groaned, and at that moment, both shyness and awe gave way, and a tenuous bond was formed. She had a single moment to look forward to an evening of eating chicken sandwiches and delving into the inner workings of his mind. Then, at the sound of a shrill whistle, she jumped, dashing coffee all over herself and over a good portion of Clay's leather covered couch in the process.

"Oh, no!" she wailed, dabbing ineffectively at the spreading liquid on the cushion beside her. "Oh, Mr. Abbott, I'm so sorry!" If the couch hadn't been built in, she'd have crawled under it.

Clay had instantly grabbed her cup, and now he was blotting her drenched body. Jo pushed his hands away. "I'm sorry, I'm so sorry," she mumbled over and over. "I should never have come here. I should never have asked for coffee."

"Are you burned? Thank God you had cream, at least it wasn't scalding. Here, let me—"

"No, please—" Her sweater was clinging to her like a lumpy second skin, and he kept trying to hold it away from her body. "I'll pay for the damages—just send me a—I've got to go," she stammered, wondering where he'd put her coat.

"You can't leave like this. Joelle, it's just a little spilled coffee, for Pete's sake, calm down. Let me get you something to put on."

"My coat," she pleaded desperately, arms clamped around her. She avoided looking at him. She avoided looking at his rug, his couch, his spattered book on the Hapsburgs, at anything. She'd probably spend the rest of her life paying for the damages, but she didn't care. All she wanted to do was get out of here and never have to face him again as long as she lived.

"Joelle, don't be foolish, I can't let you leave like this."

"You want a deposit? I'll give you everything I have, but it's not—"

"Dammit, woman, what's got into you? Forget the coffee! It's not the first time anyone spilled a drink in here and

it won't be the last. I simply meant I can't let you go anywhere soaking wet like that. If you catch pneumonia, it'll be
on my conscience.''

"You're absolved of any responsibility," she said in an
agonized tone. "Please, could I have my coat? *Please?*''

With a succinct oath, Clay wheeled away and stalked to
the coat closet, returning a moment later with the warm, if
unglamorous, jacket she'd worn for the past three years. "I
don't know what the devil your problem is, but I suggest
you learn to handle it a little better before you go knocking
on any more stranger's doors," he growled, forcing her stiff
arms into the sleeves. "Okay, Cinderella, zip up your rags
and hurry back to your nice safe hearth." The smile that
accompanied the words didn't reach the scathing brilliance
of his eyes, and she cringed, wondering how she'd managed to make such a fool of herself in such a short time. And
over nothing more serious than a cup of coffee.

"Oh, Joelle," he called after her as she darted toward the
door.

Jo hesitated, far too miserable to look back, yet wishing
it didn't have to end on such an embarrassing note. For just
a few minutes, it had been so good, she'd felt so exhila-
rated.

"You can tell your boss that if she wants an answer to her
demands, she'll have to negotiate. Through you," he
stressed.

She must have mumbled something as she yanked at the
massive doorknob, but the last thing she heard as she scur-
ried outside was another series of ear-splitting whistles.

I'll wake up in a minute, she promised herself as she
jogged over to where she'd left her car. *I'll tell Ivan all about
this wild dream I had, and we'll both have a good laugh over
breakfast.*

But Clay Abbott was no dream, she acknowledged with a sigh born of longing, frustration, and hopelessness.

"What a stupid dolt! He must think I'm ready for the butterfly net," she muttered through clenched teeth. The cold air that bit through her clothes was no match for the heat that scalded her body as she ground on the starter and wrestled with a stiff, reluctant gearshift.

Three

<hr />

You didn't get a commitment from him?" Harriet demanded. "Joella, what do you think I pay you for?"

"I'm certain he'll print it, Miss Brower," Jo said worriedly. She was certain of no such thing. All she was certain of was that once more she'd made an abject fool of herself before Clayton Abbott.

"Get the keys, we're going to that newspaper office, right now! If my petition isn't in the Sunday edition, that man is going to find himself out of a job."

"Can you do that?" Jo whispered, stunned at the thought of being held responsible, even indirectly, for a tragedy of such magnitude.

"Get the keys. Don't dawdle, girl! I do wish you'd wear something besides those disgusting dungarees. In my day, a woman dressed like a woman."

And never wore a hat without gloves, and never gloves without a hat, Jo finished silently. She knew the spiel by heart; she'd heard it often enough, but there were limits beyond which she could not be pushed.

The drive to the newspaper office took less than five minutes. Jo spent the time inventing a cast iron excuse why she should remain with the car instead of going inside.

"You wait right here, this won't take long," Harriet promised grimly. She got out of the car, adjusted her hat and tugged down her girdle. "Only way to get things done right is to do them myself," she muttered.

Parked between a flatbed truck and a lowslung sports car, the respectably middle-aged black Cadillac soaked up the February sun. Jo took off her tan wool gloves and opened her jacket. After a few moments she slipped down in the seat and closed her eyes.

She'd twisted and turned in bed until shortly before dawn, reliving every moment she'd spent in Clayton's company. In retrospect, she thought of all the bright, witty things she could have said and wondered why the Middleton gene pool of looks and brains had gone haywire the night she'd been conceived.

When the door opened, letting in a blast of cold air, she was startled out of her daydream. "He's not in," Harriet announced in deeply offended tones. "Nearly ten o'clock, and the man's not even at his desk! And that slugabed thinks he can tell *me* what's good for this town?"

With a noncommittal murmur Jo started the car again, backed out and paused at the parking lot exit to check for traffic before pulling into the street. *Please, dear Lord, let things get back to normal now. Let Harriet learn to trust the postal service, and let me stop fantasizing. Let me forget that my hero is even more stunning in the flesh than he is in print, and that he considers me about as sharp as an earthworm after a hard rain. If he thinks of me at all.*

"Take a right. You know the old MacLuckie Farm Road?"

"Miss Brower, we can't go there!" Jo exclaimed.

"Give me one good reason why not."

"Because—because we . . ." The car behind her honked, Jo's foot slipped off the brake, and the car lurched out into the street, narrowly missing a collision with a pickup truck. Mercifully, the resultant blare of horns blotted out Harriet's remarks.

All too soon, Jo found herself once more pulling up before Clayton Abbott's sprawling rock, wood and glass country home. "I'll just turn the car around while you're inside talking to Mr. Abbott," she offered helpfully.

"You'll do no such thing. You'll march up to that door and tell that man that if my petition isn't in Sunday's edition, he'll never work on another newspaper in the state of Georgia."

"Miss Brower, I can't do that!"

"Would you rather get a job waiting tables at Sharky's Seafood House?"

Jo would rather starve, and Harriet Brower knew it. It was the thought of having to deal with the public that made her go on swallowing Harriet's outrageous eccentricities year after year. That plus the fact that most of her work was done in a quiet back room in the old Brower house on Sandersted Street. There weren't many jobs in Greensport that would pay a living wage and still allow a person to remain in the background.

But this wasn't the background. Now and then Harriet went a little overboard on behalf of one of her worthy causes, but this was the first time Jo had been directly on the firing line. "The last time, too, dammit" she vowed as she stalked across the wide graveled driveway. "I wasn't hired to run your blasted errands, I was hired to type your blasted correspondence and stuff your blasted flyers in your blasted envelopes!'' She jammed her thumb against the doorbell and held it there.

Don't be home, don't be home, don't be—

"Good morning, Jo, you're looking in high spirits today."

High spirits didn't begin to describe the way Clay was looking. Jo swallowed hard, finally remembered to breathe, and then gulped again as she took in the bare chest, the leather-clad shoulders, and the broad grin. Her shocked eyes lifted to his dancing blue ones.

Leather and naked torsos? At half past ten in the morning? This was too kinky for her.

"Jo? Your mouth's open, but I don't hear anything coming out. Is something wrong? Look, come on inside and let me get a shirt on. I was getting ready to—"

"No!" Jo squawked, eyeing the scarred, rough edged slabs of leather that covered the top of both broad, muscular shoulders. In spite of the flawlessly tailored dark pants and the gleaming cordovans, he looked exotic and more than a little barbaric.

"I didn't come here alone this time," she warned. "Miss Brower's waiting out in the car."

Clay glanced beyond her. "So I see," he said grimly. "Maybe I'd better leave my armor on a bit longer." And then his gaze returned to Jo, warming with amusement and something less easily definable as it moved over her strained expression. "Jo, what's wrong?"

"Nothing's wrong. At least . . ." Warily, she let her eyes skim the ragged edges of the heavy leather garment and drop lower. He was hairy! Neither of her brothers had much hair on their chests, certainly nothing to compare with Clay's.

"Joelle? Cat got your tongue?"

"I'm sorry. I'm supposed to deliver a message." With a guilty flush, she lifted her gaze to a spot several inches above his head. Unfortunately, her peripheral vision was excellent. It was impossible to miss the puzzled lowering of his thick, straight brows, the way his mouth could remain perfectly still, yet still give the impression of smiling.

Clay stepped back, holding the door wide for her to follow. "I'll take delivery inside."

She stood rooted to the spot. "Miss Brower said—"

"Inside, Jo."

"It's a short message," she said desperately. Leather or not, there was nothing in the world she wanted more at this moment than to follow him through that door. To follow him anywhere. All the more reason why she should speak her piece and run.

"Joelle!"

"All right, all right," she yelped, practically leaping through the door.

"Let me get my shirt on and shut a few cages," Clay said, striding across the room. "I'm not partial to green stains down the back of my shirt."

Jo sighed unconsciously, gazing after him. With his broad, tanned back and that skimpy leather thing, he looked like some ancient gladiator in battle-scarred armor. Had he said *cages*? What next, for God's sake—whips and chains? What sort of man answered the door in the middle of the day wearing nothing but black pants and a scrap of leather?

So much for her secret fantasies about a gentle, courageous, learned editor, a man whose claws were the more effective for being sheathed in a droll limerick. It had probably been some deep-seated survival instinct that had made her dump her coffee and go dashing out of here the last time she'd seen him.

When Clay returned, buttoning the cuffs of a crisp white shirt, Jo was on her hands and knees, searching for any coffee stains on the Oriental rug. She scrambled to her feet and backed away. "I'm really sorry."

"For kneeling at my feet?" He finished the cuffs, but didn't bother to button the front of his shirt. Nor was he wearing an undershirt, a fact which Jo found entirely too distracting for comfort.

"For spilling coffee all over your house, for—for intruding on your privacy, for—" Gone was the threatening gladiator, in his place was the man with the gentle smile and the laughing eyes. "And for—"

Clay covered her twisting fingers with one large hand. "And for chewing your nails, and for having freckles and the loveliest eyes this side of heaven? For having the courage to tell me that you sometimes disagree with my editorial opinions, but not having the courage to tell that officious old dragon out there to take a flying leap?"

"I do?" Jo whispered.

"You do which?"

"Have lovely eyes?"

Before she could take back the revealing words, Clay caught her to him, laughing aloud. "Bless you, yes," he pronounced. "Beautiful eyes, exquisite skin, hair that could light up an arctic night."

The words, as wonderful as they were, were largely wasted on Jo. Locked in his arms, her nostrils filled with the clean masculine scent of him, every nerve between her knees and her shoulders reeled drunkenly from the unexpected contact. She could only do her best to hang on and hope the earth would soon settle back into a normal orbit.

Clay laughed again, more softly this time. His hands moved up and down her back, seeking some hint of what lay beneath all the layers of clothing. There was a lot to be said for the spontaneous gesture, he decided. At the rate they'd been progressing, it would have taken him six months to get this far, and he couldn't wait that long.

It was a crazy reaction, one he made no attempt to understand. He'd played the game with experts, and he prided himself on being a skilled and generous player. But Joelle Middleton obviously didn't even know the name of the game, much less the rules. That was no seductive perfume she was wearing, that was Joelle and plain old soap. She probably used the unscented variety. There was nothing faintly alluring about the shapeless, colorless clothes she wore, and yet Clay felt a physical response so powerful and so immediate that he was at a loss to explain it.

As his hardening body blithely ignored the admonitions of his brain, he shifted uncomfortably. He didn't want to scare her off, yet he couldn't bring himself to push her away. Not just yet.

He barely knew the woman. She was so awkward she couldn't talk to a man without coloring like a stoplight, and she was driving him wild!

"Joelle?" he murmured tentatively. Didn't she know what she was doing to him? Surely she wasn't that naive.

"Clayton, I'm sor—"

"If you apologize one more time—for *anything*—you're going to find yourself in serious trouble."

But not as much trouble as he was in, Clay told himself helplessly as she wriggled in his embrace. He'd heard of spontaneous combustion, but this was ridiculous! His arms tightened around her and he closed his eyes and buried his face in that wild and wonderful blaze of hair she tried so unsuccessfully to tame.

Jo was breathlessly aware of what was happening. She was much less certain of how it had happened. And why. And what to do about it. One thing she did know—her instincts wouldn't be any help to her this time. She could see the headlines now: "Sex-crazed Secretary Attacks Erudite Editor."

Her eyelids were growing heavier by the moment, and she was experiencing distinct difficulties with her breathing. As for the heat that was uncoiling in the pit of her stomach like a charmed serpent, she had a feeling that it was going to get a lot worse before it got better.

What did a woman do in a case like this? Dear Lord, they were practically strangers. Of course, he didn't seem like a stranger. He didn't feel like a stranger, either, with the hard warmth of his arms wrapped around her and the musky scent of his body filling her nostrils as she buried her face in his throat.

But what had *he* been thinking of? What had made him reach out to her that way? A painfully shy beanpole practically all her life, Jo had never been accused of leading a man on.

Had she led him on? Was that why he was hanging on to her as if he'd never let her go? More likely, he was afraid she'd do something crazy if he turned her loose.

"Clay, you don't have to hold me any longer," she said shakily. "I might be a klutz, but I'm not actually dangerous."

"You're sure? I'm beginning to have my doubts," he said, his voice no steadier than hers had been. It occurred to him to wonder what she'd have done with her arms if he hadn't trapped her against him, pinning them both at her sides. Would she have wound them around his neck? How he'd love to feel her arms around him, her hands on his naked body. At the thought, he felt a leaping response, and he groaned and forced his mind into some semblance of control.

He eased his grip reluctantly, one hand lingering on her arm, and Jo moved away. But before she could escape completely, a shriek from the depths of the house sent her hurtling back to the security of his embrace.

"What *is* that?" she cried, her fists crushing what had been a crisply laundered shirt only a moment before.

Never one to question fate, Clay pressed her tightly against him once more and valiantly fought his libido to a standstill. "Don't be afraid, it's only Rudy. He resents having his morning exercise interrupted."

"Rudy? The cage?"

"Rudy's a parrot, an African Gray. Pretty spoiled, I'm afraid."

"Then that explains the other night, that terrible scream just as I was leaving."

"Sounds like Rudy. I don't even hear him half the time now, I'm so used to it." Clay's fingers strayed up to the wild thicket of hair that was constrained into a thick braid. "He does a terrific wolf whistle, by the way. I taught him everything he knows."

Her face still pressed against his throat, Jo smiled, and then began to laugh, remembering the chaotic feelings that had followed her through the door that night. "It could have been a pack of wolves, and I wouldn't have known the difference. Clay, I was so embarrassed."

Easing one hand between their two bodies, Clay accidentally encountered the soft swell of one small breast. Wincing, he jerked his hand away and brought it up under her chin, tilting her face to his. "Of course you were," he said gravely when he could trust himself to speak. "No one to my knowledge has ever spilled coffee before. At least not in this part of the world. There once was a man from Lahore, who spilled a full cup on the floor." His eyes took on a wicked gleam as he searched for an acceptable ending. "I've oft heard it said, they offed with his head, but that's only—"

"A wicked rumore," Jo finished, delighted for once that her wits hadn't altogether abandoned her.

"You like limericks?"

She nodded, feeling a glow of accomplishment all out of proportion to merely having finished one he'd begun. "Clayton?" she whispered when the glow began to fade.

"Yes, Joelle?"

"I really don't think we should be standing here. I mean, like this."

Immediately, one of Clay's hands dropped to cup her hips, while the other one slipped up to cradle the back of her head. He stared down at her with mock seriousness. "Is this better?"

Rudy's distinctive voice penetrated the warm fog that was creeping into Jo's brain like morning mist over the Savannah River. *Clayton? Whut! Clayton? Whut!*

"Damned illiterate bird," Clay muttered.

"I think you probably should release me, Clayton," she whispered.

"There once was a woman named Jo, and a man who couldn't let go." His arms loosened fractionally, but his eyes held her fast with their laughter.

Jo reluctantly began to extricate herself. "This is embarrassing. I've never done anything like this before, Clayton," she said in a barely audible voice.

"Completed a limerick, you mean?"

"Oh, I do that all the time. Sometimes I even rewrite one of yours."

"Then what haven't you done, Joelle? Kissed a man?"

"Not in ages and ages." When the words sank in her eyes widened. "But I'm not kissing you," she protested just as his lips brushed the tip of her nose. Still staring, she saw his face tilt to one side, saw the darkness eclipse the blue of his eyes. The last of her reason melted, and she became aware of the crash of thunder, the pound of a storm-driven surf.

Was it her own heart? His?

In that last moment, her lips parted to accept the warm, moist pressure of his. When she felt the tip of his tongue begin to explore the line between her lips, seeking entrance, her knees buckled. It was a good thing she was hanging on for dear life, for her strength fled, leaving her a trembling shell.

"Joella? I demand to know what's going on in there! Open that door this minute!"

"Oh, no!" Jo wailed.

"Oh, hell," Clay swore.

"Joella!" Harriet pounded on the door once more, at the same time ringing the doorbell. "I'll give you one minute to come out of there before I go for help."

Jo swayed as Clayton removed his arms to stride to the door. He swung it open and faced the stout angry woman in mink. "Miss Brower, if you have anything to say to me, you're free to call my secretary and make an appointment at any time during business hours."

"Decent folks go to work at a decent hour. Do you know what time it is?"

"You came out here just to ask me the time?" Clay's voice held an edge that made Jo shiver.

"Where is my secretary? What have you done with her?"

"She's in my bed, naturally, and I appreciate your generosity, but Harry, I think I should tell you—as a rule, I don't accept bribes."

Jo uttered a sound that was halfway between a scream and a moan. "Clay, please!" Grabbing his hand, she tugged him aside and darted past, coming face to face with her apoplectic employer. "Miss Brower, he was only teasing. Please, there's nothing— Dammit, Clay, tell her! Miss Brower, let me explain—there was this bird, an African Gray, and—''

"Joelle, if you think you're capable of getting us home again, I suggest you stop babbling and get yourself into the car. We'll see about this later."

Clay called just before she left work that afternoon. "Joelle? Just wanted to apologize for embarrassing you. The woman ticks me off."

Jo covered the phone and sent an agonized glance at Harriet. "Who is that?" the older woman demanded suspiciously.

"I can't talk now, Clay, but everything's all right. You—uh, you will put the petition in the Sunday paper, won't you?" she asked apologetically. She was sick of the damned petition, sick of Harriet and her everlasting troublemaking, and sick, most of all, of being such a lily-livered wimp!

"Tell your boss that if she'll agree to debate me on the issue at an open town meeting, I'll print her damned petition and the signature of every citizen listed, living or dead."

Jo hung up and passed on the message, shrinking from the predictable reaction. Harriet flew into a fine rage, and Jo listened in miserable silence until the massive grandfather clock in the foyer bonged five times. Then she collected her coat and purse and let herself out the side door. Enough was enough, even for a wimp.

Sybil called in the middle of her supper. "Hi, hon—you in the middle of anything?"

"Soup and crackers."

"How does smoked turkey sound? With dilled potato salad and baked apples?"

"Who do I have to kill?" Jo was a little wary of her older sister's invitations. She was also a little wary of her brother-in-law, Oscar, having fallen in love with him in about the tenth grade. Jo had never been sure whether or not Oscar had told Sybil about that day in the grape arbor, the summer of her junior year in high school, when she'd blurted out her pent-up feelings. He'd turned brick red, muttered something about loving her like a little sister, and then Sybil had come to find them.

"There you are!" she'd exclaimed. "I've been looking everywhere, Joelle. Has Oscar told you yet? Isn't it exciting? How would you like to be a bridesmaid?"

Jo had been a bridesmaid. She hadn't liked it. Over the intervening years, she'd recovered from her early passion, but it had been ages before she could bring herself to relax in Oscar's presence.

"Are you offering supper?" she asked now.

"Depends. Are you available?" Sybil countered. In the background, Jo could hear two-year-old Shannon demanding her favorite snack of "tseese 'n' cackas."

"Well . . . sure. I'll see if I can get out of the dinner cruise with the Argentinian polo player. Polo players are all so boringly predictable."

"I keep telling you," Sybil Turner said with the brutal frankness of an older sister, "get your hair cut and buy yourself some new clothes. Did Fran show you that little black suit? You could let out the skirt and—"

"What time?" Jo interrupted. She wasn't in the mood for another sisterly lecture of self-improvement.

"Tomorrow night? Around six would suit us if it suits you. That'll give you some time to play with Shannon before she goes to bed."

Jo hung up, torn between elation and depression. She'd never considered herself an emotional person, but she was beginning to wonder. Her social life was nil, except for her family. She watched TV, read a lot, argued with editors and anchormen, and confided not in relatives, but in a bird. Of course, there was Mike, Harriet's nephew. They'd gone out several times, but that hardly counted. The only reason Jo didn't break it off was that Mike was even more of a social misfit than she was, and she felt sorry for him.

Now and then she even found herself resenting the successful lives of her brothers and sisters, which was ridiculous. She refused to admit to being jealous of her own family, just because their lives were so much more fulfilling than hers.

Chip, at forty-one, and with hair only slightly less red than hers, was a co-owner of the biggest auto-supply store in Greensport. Hal, the baby, dark like their father and a real winner with women, had gone to school three years on an athletic scholarship and dropped out to manage a sporting goods place near Augusta. As for her sisters, one older, one younger, both were beautiful, happily married to successful professional men, and Fran was a pharmacist as well.

But there were times when Jo was sick to death of every last one of them, for no better reason than that they were all so perfect, with their lovely noisy homes and their lovely noisy families and their lovely...

"You're coming down with something," Joelle grumbled. Ivan dutifully assumed his listening stance, and Jo laughed tiredly. "What d'you think, Ive—a new dress? A haircut? Remember the last time I let someone try to do something with this mop? I looked like I'd jammed my toe into a light socket."

Jo arrived at work the following day to discover that Harriet had espoused another worthy cause, that of closing down the town's only so-called adult book store and the maroon cinder-block building behind it that bore a sign boasting an All-Girl Staff.

"Does this mean the Voegler house is—"

"It means nothing of the sort," Harriet informed her. "Do you have any idea what goes on in places like that?"

"The Voegler house?"

"Don't be impertinent, girl, you know perfectly well what I'm talking about."

Jo wisely decided against asking if Harriet herself knew the purpose of the all-girl staff. "What about the debate?"

"Debate? What debate? If you think I'm going to demean myself by getting into a public brawl with some snooping reporter, you're very much mistaken. Call Abbott and tell him that unless he prints my petition along with every single signature, I'll go straight to his publisher. Believe me, I'm not without influence in this town."

"But isn't the Greensport Daily owned by a publisher from Atlant—"

"Joella!"

"Yes, Miss Brower," Jo muttered meekly, ducking her head and pretending to search in the desk drawer.

"Well? What are you waiting for? Call and tell them what I said!"

Jo dialed Clay's office, intending to give the message to his secretary and hang up. To her dismay, Clay answered the phone. Jo's mouth opened, and her brain promptly blew a fuse. She couldn't for the life of her remember what it was she'd called to say.

"Joelle? Is that you?"

"How did you know?" she asked weakly.

"I'm beginning to recognize your style. I was planning to call you later."

"You were?"

"Joella," Harriet said warningly, and Jo gripped the phone until her fingertips whitened.

"Look, Mr. Abbott, what I called about was—uh, well, Miss Brower doesn't believe a debate would be in the public interest."

"Screw Miss Brower," Clay said succinctly. "Look, Jo, how about dinner tonight? I know a small quiet place where we could cap each other's limericks to our heart's content."

"Oh, Clay," Jo sighed, ignoring the glowering face across her neat desk. "I'd love to, but I promised my sister I'd go there for smoked turkey. Oscar smokes them himself, and they're delicious."

"Hmmm, I'll bet they are, but how are Oscar's limericks?"

Jo giggled. Harriet snorted and grabbed for the phone, but this time, Jo held her ground. "You could come, too, Clay—if you'd like to. Sybil won't mind. Dinner's usually pretty hectic with a two-year-old in the house."

"I'm partial to two-year-olds. You've got yourself a deal. Pick you up at home after work, okay?"

By the time Harriet succeeded in wresting the phone away, the line was dead. She slammed it down. "Would you mind telling me what that was all about? Have you lost your mind?"

"Miss Brower, I'm sorry, it won't happen again." Jo did her best to look suitably chastised as Harriet went on about decent girls and gratitude and unreliable help, but it was difficult. She hugged her joy inside her where it was safe, waiting until she got home to let it burst free.

"Ivan, Ivan, you lovely little lovebird, he's asked me out," she sang. Whirling around her tiny living room, she tossed her coat in one direction, her gloves and purse in another.

The lovebird looked distinctly unimpressed, and she opened his cage and crooned to him, allowing him to step off onto her finger and walk up her arm. At the prickle of his tiny claws, she thought about the leather garment Clay had been wearing.

Parrots. That explained it, then. Although he weighed only a few ounces, Ivan was capable of inflicting real damage. She wasn't familiar with African Grays, but they were bound to be larger, and a larger bird could easily injure a man. Some parrots she'd heard of had a grip like the Jaws-of-Life.

"He's coming to pick me up, Ive," she chanted, and then it occurred to her that she hadn't given him her address. But then, Clay was a newspaperman. Newspapermen always had their sources. He'd find her, and when he did, she'd do her best to make him glad he'd taken the trouble. She was proud of her whole family; Sybil was beautiful and charming, and Oscar's smoked turkey was out of this world, and Shannon could win the heart of a wooden Indian.

Jo's best dress was a dark green wool jersey with an ivory linen collar. Thank God low heels were momentarily in style again as she was capable of turning her ankles walking across a bare floor in sneakers. In high heels, she was a disaster.

After a quick shower, she took down her braid and brushed her hair until it stood out around her head like a neon Medusa. Then, with practiced fingers, she quickly rebraided it and coiled the braid on top of her head, anchoring it securely. Her pearl earrings were fake, but then, she'd never been able to tell the difference between those and the real ones her other brother-in-law, Pete, had given Fran for her twenty-fifth birthday.

She sniffed the bottle of perfume Chip's wife had passed on to her Christmas before last. Someone had given it to Candy, and she'd tried it and hadn't cared for it. "Yuk!" Jo wrinkled her nose and recapped the bottle. Some things obviously didn't improve with age.

By the time her buzzer rang, she was ready to peel off her dress, shroud herself in a quilt, and claim a sudden case of Peruvian flu. What on earth had she been thinking about, inviting a strange man to meet her family on the first date? At that rate, the first date would also be the last. Even Sybil had sounded a little startled when Jo had called to ask if she could bring along a friend.

"A friend?"

"Actually, he's sort of a—a man. A date, you might say."

"Well...sure. I suppose so. I mean, there's certainly plenty of food on hand. Oscar smoked three whole turkeys and two breasts yesterday. I froze all but this one breast— seven pounds, two ounces, on special for fifty-nine cents a pound—and when the Handleys called, I was tempted to stick this one in the freezer, too, but—"

Jo had been in no mood to listen to a recital of her sister's thought processes. Sybil had total recall of everything that had happened to her from the moment of birth. The birth had been dramatic. The price of turkey was not.

"Wish me luck," she whispered to Ivan as she opened the door to Clay's knock.

"Oh, geez." Clay rocked back on his heels, staring in open admiration, and Jo felt herself coloring. She ducked her head.

"Come on in," she said. "Don't mind me—I'm not really feverish, I just happen to have thin skin."

"You look like an old-fashioned Christmas card." Clay stepped inside her apartment, taking in the modest furnishings, the jungle of house plants and the large bird cage with one swift glance. "You're a bird person, too? Why didn't you say so?"

Jo, her twisting fingers clasped behind her, watched as he approached Ivan's cage. He didn't make the mistake most people did of thinking that just because a bird was small and colorful, he was also quite harmless. "Ivan's a Fischer Lovebird. I've had him for about four years now."

"Hand raised?"

"Not my hand. My sister gave him to me. Not the sister we're having dinner with tonight, but my other sister. Fran bought him to go with the jungle printed draperies in her sun room, but after he pierced Pete's ear and took a bite out of her finger, she decided to settle for a large Strelitzia and a few showy Bromelia plants."

"Ivan the Terrible?"

"I think of him as Ivanhoe, but he does have his moments. He doesn't like men."

Clay grinned broadly. "Thanks for the warning. Are we ready to go?"

The drive to the Turner's impressive new home took just over ten minutes. Jo, already beginning to regret her impulsive invitation, slipped off a glove and lifted a finger to her teeth.

"Nervous?" Clay asked quietly, and guiltily, she dropped her fist to her lap.

"Yes. I don't usually—I didn't tell them who you were, and—"

"You're afraid they won't like me?"

"Oh, no," Jo said quickly, amazed that he could even harbor the thought. "I meant—well, I don't usually invite my dates to meet my family the first time." Up went the fingers again, and she searched for a shred of nail. "I didn't mean I expect this to be the first—what I meant was . . ."

Clay's hand closed over hers and he brought it to his lips and kissed the tips of her non-existent nails. Jo could have died on the spot.

"Relax, Joelle. I promise to be on my best behavior, company table manners and all, and if your family's anything at all like you, I'm going to love them."

Four

Sybil had always looked good in Autumn Haze mink. It matched her hair. Only Jo wasn't wondering about the impression her family was making on Clayton Abbott at the moment. She was wondering why her sister was wearing a full-length fur to answer the door.

"My goodness," Sybil said blankly, staring up at Clayton, who looked even more magnificent than usual in a dark, faintly tweedy gray suit with a wine-colored vest. "Oh, my goodness, where did Jo find you?"

"Sybil?" Jo felt like waving a hand in front of her sister's face to break the spell. "Isn't this the night? Smoked turkey? The Handleys? Us?"

"The Handleys—oh. Right!" said Sybil brightly. "Come in, you two. I'm Sybil Turner, Jo's sister, and you're...?"

Jo, harboring the seeds of a dreadful suspicion, finished the introductions just as Oscar came into the room carrying a topcoat on one arm and two-year-old Shannon on the other. "My, my, aren't *you* all gussied up tonight! Hardly recognized you. Sorry about the short notice, hon, but the regular sitter busted her ankle with a bowling ball. If you'd told us you had a date with Clayton Abbott, we'd have planned to stay home." Without giving Jo a chance to speak, he turned to Clay. "Abbott, real glad to meet you. That piece you ran on the new landfill site was a dilly! Few red faces at the last county commissioners meeting, huh? So ol' Jo managed to rope you into baby-sitting tonight, huh? Better watch out or she'll talk your ears off. Never could shut 'er up, myself, that's why I had to settle for Silent Sybil."

Arsenic, Oscar, administered over a long period of time. I want it to be slow and agonizing. Jo turned to her sister, eyes glittering a little too brightly. "Has Shannon eaten yet? Did she have a nap?"

"Yes and no, in that order. I left the turkey out, but the salad's in the fridge. You can take a couple of baked apples out of the freezer and pop them in the microwave. There's whipped cream if you want it, but you'd better sniff it first—I bought it for last Sunday's peach cobbler."

"Thank you, Sybil." If her smile looked a bit forced, it was only because she'd never been so furious in her life.

"Nant Jo, weed my book?"

"Yes, darling, Nant Jo will read your book." She stroked her niece's chubby legs and tried not to look at Clay. It was probably the first time in his life he'd been invited out on a baby-sitting date.

She was tempted to walk out of the house and just keep going. Forever and ever, until everyone forgot she'd ever existed.

What ever happened to whatsername?

Who?

Weren't there five of those Middleton kids? I seem to re-member...

Naah, you just imagined it.

It would have been different if she hadn't been fool enough to invite Clay along to witness her ignominy. She was always being called in to look after her nieces and nephews. She loved it, only why couldn't they come right out and ask her to baby-sit instead of trying to sugar coat it by making it sound like something else.

Just last winter she'd been invited for a weekend at the beach. Chip and Candy, Fran and Pete, and Syb and Oscar had rented an enormous cottage at St. Simons for a whole week, and Hal and Jo were included. Hal had begged off, but Jo had gone out and bought bathing suits, sun dresses, and even a gauzy full length skirt.

She might as well have saved her money. Fran's Petey had blistered the first day, and from then on, Jo had stayed at the cottage with him and Chessie, his baby sister, Shannon, who'd been only a year old, and Chip, Jr., who'd been twelve then. The others had raced sailboats all day, and then celebrated far into the night at the local yacht club.

Jo heartily wished her family would do her the courtesy of telling her in plain language when they needed a baby-sitter and when they wanted her company. It wasn't that she resented being used; what she resented was the resentment she always felt afterward.

Her smile, when she saw the two of them out a few minutes later, was little more than a grimace, and even that faded the minute the door closed behind them. Still holding Shannon, who was fascinated with the pins that held her braid in place, she took a deep breath and started in on her apology. "I'm sorry, Clay. It was my fault for misunderstanding. I just don't know what to say except—I'm sorry."

"What are you sorry for this time, Joelle?"

"Please, don't make it any worse," she said miserably. "I feel like a big enough idiot already. It isn't their fault, it's mine. I'm always jumping to conclusions." She swallowed the painful lump in her throat and willed herself not to blush, not to cry, not to do anything undignified.

"Aren't you overreacting a bit?"

"Look, I thought we were invited to dinner with some people named Handley, but as usual, I got my signals crossed. Syb and Oscar were invited out with the Handleys. I was invited to look after Shannon, and you—"

"And I was wondering how I was going to get you alone with all those people around." Clay leaned against the impeccable white mantel with its impeccably correct accessories. It was pretty obvious what had happened; even more obvious that she was embarrassed about it; but hell, it was a simple mistake. Anyone else would have laughed it off. Clay studied the woman before him, her striking coloring underlined by the deep-green and ivory dress. With that golden-haired bundle of energy in her arms, she could have modeled for one of the Old Masters.

For the life of him, he couldn't figure out why such a woman should be so lacking in self-confidence. But he was damned well going to find out.

There was no escaping the searching intensity of his gaze. Miserably, Jo wondered what he was thinking. That she was a pathetic doormat? She was. That she'd inveigled him here under false pretenses? She had, but not intentionally. "Clay, it's still early. If you have something else to do," she offered, torn between wanting him to go and wanting him to stay, "I certainly don't expect you to—"

He broke in impatiently. "I was promised smoked turkey."

"Oh. Well, that's still available, I guess. Oscar does do marvelous turkeys." Capturing a small, chubby fist, she removed it from her hair. "Darling, don't pull out my hair-pins. Nant Jo's hair will run wild if we let it escape."

Slipping off his coat, Clay reached out his arms, and the child toppled forward as if she'd known him all her young life. "Leave Nant Jo's hair to me, angel. If it's going to run wild, I want to be in at the starting line."

While he entertained Shannon with limericks about a cat named Louise who only ate cheese, and a dog named McDiddle, who danced to a fiddle, Jo sliced turkey and spread thick sandwiches.

"Milk?" she asked, peering in the refrigerator.

"Beer?"

"I'll see." She removed two frosty bottles of Oscar's imported brew and sat them on the kitchen table.

"I think someone's getting sleepy," Clay suggested with a meaningful look at the drowsy child in his arms.

Jo glanced up and sighed. "Send me your dry-cleaning bill, will you? Unless that happens to be a needlepoint vest done in a random cheese-and-cracker-crumb pattern."

"She was hungry, the little sweetheart," Clay murmured. "Do we change her clothes before we put her down, or tuck her in as is?"

"I'll do it, you go ahead and eat."

"Hey, don't hog all the fun for yourself. Lead on, I'll carry her."

Together they wiped, changed, and bedded the sleepy child down, meeting with little more than the perfunctory protest.

"Nant Jo and Cay," Clay repeated, smiling as they went back downstairs. "Sounds kind of cozy, huh?"

"You're a natural. You must have had lots of practice." Jo couldn't bring herself to ask outright about his personal life, but she'd been wondering all evening about the ease with which Clay had handled the situation.

"Nope. Only child of an only child." He opened both bottles of beer, searched cabinets until he located glasses, and after carefully pouring, handed her one. "And none of my own, in case you were wondering."

She colored, but only the palest shade of fuchsia. She was learning not to react like a weather vane to the slightest implication. "I wasn't," she said quickly, and then, "Yes I was."

They took their sandwiches and beer into the living room, and Jo put on a tape to fill in any awkward silences. As it turned out, neither of them heard much of the music. Clay told her what it was like growing up an only child, first on a series of army bases, and then in a household of adults that included his parents and an elderly aunt.

"I learned to read early, probably so I'd have something to pass the time while I waited for permission to speak. My father was career Army, very big on the 'speak-when-you're-spoken-to' school of behavior."

"My mother was a disc jockey and my father was an insurance agent. In our house, it was more a case of speak when you can fit a word in edgeways."

"Why do I get the impression that you didn't bother to try very hard?"

Jo slid the plate with the last sandwich toward him, and Clay sliced it neatly in two, handing her half. "Oh...I never had anything really worth saying, I suppose. My family, well, Mamma and Daddy are both gone now, but all my brothers and sisters are big achievers. There was always something going on in our house. Chip and Hal were both football stars, and Chip coached basketball for the recreation department up until last year when he slipped a disc. Fran's a pharmacist and part owner of a drugstore, and Sybil was a runner-up in the Miss Georgia pageant. She was in the finals for the state piano competition when she was fifteen, too."

"And Joelle?" Jo's smile would have been lost if Clay hadn't reached across the table and lifted her chin until her eyes met his. "What about the middle Middleton?"

"Oh, that one? Nothing special—B-minus average, no college, no sports, no beauty pageants, no special talent. Pretty practical, though. At least she had the good sense to take a business course."

"Are we talking about the same Middleton? Named after a relative who lost a fortune in pork bellies, works for the toughest broad in town?"

"She sounds vaguely familiar," she said, laughter gurgling just under the surface.

"Sure she does. World class ankles, incandescent hair, eyes a man could drown in, and skin as soft as the sigh of a butterfly."

Carefully, Jo laid down her sandwich, blotted her lips, and covered her face with her hands. "Clay, please don't talk that way," she groaned. "You're embarrassing me. I know you're only joking, but I'd much rather talk about—about your work," she finished in a desperate flurry of words.

Gently, Clay removed her hands from her face. At the sight of her imploring gaze, he felt as if he'd just lifted a newly hatched bird from the nest. "Joelle," he murmured, rising to come around the coffee table. He dropped down onto the arm of her chair, placing a hand on her shoulder to keep her from escaping. "Jo, what is it? What's wrong? Are you afraid of me, is that it? Do I offend you?"

At the thought of such heresy, she quickly looked up. "Oh, no! You could never offend anyone, Clay," she said so earnestly it was all he could do not to sweep her into his arms.

"I can name several dozen people who'd disagree with you," he suggested with a rueful smile, "but if that's not the case, then why do you keep running away?"

"I'm not running. That is, not exactly." Scrupulously honest, she did her best to explain. "I'm just not very good with people. I never was. It isn't that I don't like them—at least most of them, but..."

"You're shy?" he prompted when she ran out of words.

Miserably, she nodded. "It's probably environmental, something to do with my background. On the other hand, Fran, Sybil, Hal and Chip grew up in the same household that I did, and they're all perfectly normal, so that theory doesn't hold water."

"There's nothing wrong with being shy." Still seated on the arm of her chair, Clay pressed her head against his side. Gradually, his arm found its way around her shoulders, and Jo, her face downcast, studied the diagonal weave of the woolen material that stretched across his lean, hard thigh.

"I read an article once that said shyness was an inherited trait, like left-handedness or an ear for music," she ventured. "But neither of my parents was shy. In fact, I don't remember anyone in the family ever being shy."

"Another leaky theory? The shyness gene would naturally be recessive."

Jo looked up, caught the twinkle in his eyes, and smiled. "Naturally," she echoed gravely. "Speaking of leaky theories, once an astrologer told me it was because I had a twelfth house sun, and that when I progressed far enough, I'd come into my own."

"Did you?" Clay reached for her hand and laced his fingers between hers.

"I'm still waiting," she replied. "Parts of me are making progress. I can hold my own with Ivan, at least. Today Ivan, tomorrow the world."

Clay laughed wholeheartedly, and after a moment, Jo joined in. He said softly,

> "There once was a lady, I'm told,
> Who was shy and considered quite cold.
> It might have been true,
> But by age eighty-two,
> She was dreadfully, shamefully bold."

Eyes sparkling, Jo shook her head admiringly. "You're quick."

"Practice," Clay said modestly. "Care to have a go at it?"

"I'd be too intimidated." She was also becoming excruciatingly aware of his nearness, of the smell of good woolens, a crisp, light scent, and an underlying note of warm masculinity that was playing havoc with her breathing.

"You don't have to wait until you're eighty-two, Jo," he said, his voice a shade huskier than before.

"I'm working on it, honestly I am."

Clay's thumb began to stroke the delicate tendon at the side of her throat, causing a ripple of pleasure to shoot through her body. Jo moved restlessly and tried to slip her hand from his, but he refused to release her.

"Jo, look at me." The hand on her throat moved to tilt her head back until she was gazing helplessly into his eyes. "Let me help," he urged gently.

She couldn't even breathe, much less speak. This must be what free-fall was like, this spiraling, tumbling, hurtling into a blueness so deep and clear that there was no end to it. She felt herself being half lifted from the chair, crushed in his arms, and then she felt the touch of his lips on hers. Her whole existence was focused on that single moment in time. It was as if they were bathed in a light of such blinding radiance that the rest of the world simply fell away into darkness.

Shuddering to restrain the driving desire that had struck him with no warning, Clay clutched the soft fabric of her dress, feeling the sweat spring out on his palms, his back. God, what was wrong with him? He was thirty-six years old, not some adolescent bedeviled by too many hormones and too little experience!

There was no shyness in evidence now, just an incredibly sweet openness that had him hanging onto control by a mere thread. The taste of her, the scent of her, the feel of all that fragile loveliness under his hands was driving him too far, too fast.

Jo sensed his withdrawal a split-second before he lifted his lips from hers. Unconsciously, she strained upward, wanting to prolong the moment. When his lips lifted, hers were still tingling from the feel of his kisses, the electrifying caress of his tongue.

"Darling, we'd better slow down," Clay whispered hoarsely, putting her away from him with hands that were none too steady.

She wilted like a flower cut down in the field and left there under a blistering sun. "I'm sorry." The words were barely audible, spoken in a haze of pain as she turned her flaming face away.

"Oh, no. Jo, it's not what you think." His hands were almost rough as he captured her face and turned her to meet his gaze. "Jo, please listen to me," he pleaded. "I didn't mean for this to happen. At least not like this." And then, seeing the dull look of defeat on her face, he groaned and tried again. "Jo, dammit—don't you know *anything*?"

Wrenching herself from his grasp, she stood and began carefully brushing nonexistent wrinkles from her dress, each small movement as tightly controlled as if she were a mechanical toy that had been wound too tightly. Dear God, any minute now her mainspring was going to fly apart, and she'd fall into a crumpled heap.

Jaws clenched in frustration, Clay watched as she carefully gathered up the sandwich plate, the glasses and napkins and took them to the kitchen, her narrow feet moving silently on the pale plush carpet. The small sounds that followed, the clink of glass, the rush of water, should have been reassuring, yet somehow they weren't. He swore softly.

Pacing the fashionably decorated room, its expensive appointments so different from the cheerful clutter of her small apartment, he wondered whether or not he'd be doing them both a favor to leave now. Sooner or later their paths would cross again in a place as small as Greensport, but by that time he might have gained a little perspective.

It was wholly out of character, Clay told himself. Sure, he liked women, always had. He'd never pretended to be a saint, but he'd never deliberately set out to seduce an innocent who hadn't the faintest idea of what it was all about.

God, where had she been all her life? She had to be at least twenty-five, yet where men were concerned—and damned near everyone else—she was totally defenseless. In this day and age, that just wasn't possible . . . was it? A man didn't fool around with a woman like that, not unless he was willing to make a commitment.

Hell, he'd never even given it a thought. Not that he had anything in particular against marriage. It had just never figured in his plans. His parents' marriage had been a pretty joyless affair. He'd learned years ago that his father had been notorious for his mistresses, and he'd been sorry for his mother's sake. But then, for as long as he could remember, as they'd moved from post to post, his mother had found compensation in alcohol and gambling.

Neither of them had been particularly interested in their only child. After his father had retired, they'd moved into the big, barren house that belonged to his aunt, and the tension had only increased. It had grown worse as Clay steadfastly refused to follow his father into the army.

He'd left home the day he'd graduated from high school, served a hitch in the navy, and then got the first of a series of jobs. Over the next several years, he'd earned a degree in journalism, and from there he'd tackled every phase of newspaper work, never staying long in one place.

There had been women along the way, some of them pretty special, but none who had even tempted him to settle down. Ironically, it was an old army buddy of his father's who was responsible for his being where he was today. Clay had been working in Augusta as editorial page editor when he'd run into Jack Kubacek. Jack had retired as a full colonel and was in the process of building a house in Greensport where he'd planned to raise Videlia onions and African Grays.

With the house practically finished, he'd found himself urgently needed in Denver to help a newly widowed daughter hang onto her business. Finding a buyer for an unfinished house with a built-in aviary and three breeding pairs of parrots was not something that could be done overnight.

It had taken Clay longer to make the necessary financial arrangements than it had to make up his mind, but he'd never regretted the decision. Over the years, he'd learned to trust his instincts. He'd learned that when he wanted something, he'd better go after it or risk losing it to someone else.

Which brought him back to the woman who was still hiding in the kitchen. The question was, should he run now while he still had the chance, or should he go with his gut feelings and see where they led him?

* * *

As it turned out, the question had been largely rhetorical. The Turners had returned while Jo was still messing about in the kitchen, and she'd refused to be drawn out on the drive home. Difficult woman! Clay, irritated, had made up his mind that the next move would be up to her.

It was for the best, he rationalized as he slogged away at his cluttered desk over the next few days and worked with that irreverent hellion, Rudy, each evening.

Hi, guys, wanna Coors?

"No, you turkey, I don't want a Coors. Get off my back until I get this place cleaned up, will you?" Rudy had picked up a pretty extensive vocabulary from the TV set Clay left on during the day to keep him company. He was beginning to suspect the bird was capable of changing channels if he didn't care for a particular program. "You're supposed to eat these grapes, not play football with them," he grumbled.

Play ball, play ball. Clayton? Whut!

"Why couldn't you have inherited a little shyness?"

The silvery-gray bird stretched his neck, fanned his red tail, and managed to look offended, and Clay relented and offered his arm to be tasted, tested, and mounted. "Come aboard, old fellow, and mind those toenails of yours. You already owe me two shirts."

Absently teasing the black bill, he thought back to the day when he'd answered the door in his leather shoulder guard. Rudy seldom required it now, but he'd been working with one of the younger birds that had not yet learned to trust him completely.

Poor Jo. She'd looked at him as if he were some sort of barbarian, and he'd been tempted to play along with her fears for a moment.

Not a word from her all week long. No word from Harriet, either. Once on the way home from work, he'd passed Jo's car, and he'd thought about turning around and following her, but he'd thought better of it.

Things hadn't gotten any better. It was still there, whatever it was that kept her on his mind. He found himself fantasizing about kidnapping her, barring the doors, and spending long, delicious nights making love to her.

But first he'd have to peel away all those layers of shyness. Hiding underneath it all there was a witty, intelligent woman who deserved to be free. What made it so maddening was that each time he caught a glimpse of that woman, she ducked away before he could get his hands on her and draw her out.

Five

"Sorry, Jo can't come to thē phone right now, she's with child," Hal said, blithely ignoring his sister's frantic signals.

Joelle, who was on her knees in the bathroom supervising Shannon's and Chessie's bath, shouted over her shoulder. "Who is it?"

"Do I get the car?"

"All right, all right, blackmailer, but who's on the phone? Is it Mike?"

"You mean Harriet's little boy?"

"He's her nephew, and he's not a little boy, now come on, Hal, stop teasing. Who is it?" If it was Mike Brower, she was just as glad she hadn't answered; Mike could be as tedious in his own way as Harriet was.

"Dunno. Whoever it was hung up when I said you couldn't come to the phone. Sounded sort of surprised, though. Hey, look, I'll fill up the tank for you before I bring it back, okay?'' Hal's 'Vette had given out just when he had an important date. As everyone else in the family had left for Atlanta, he'd been reduced to borrowing Jo's less-than-glamorous sedan.

"And rotate my tires?"

"Anything else?" The good-looking ex-athlete heaved an exaggerated sigh.

"Just be careful, I know how fast you like to drive."

"In that clunker of yours? Say, what about Mike? Think he'd care to share his wheels with a future brother-in-law?"

Jo threw a soggy sponge tugboat at him and missed, and Chessie, giggling, immediately began throwing toys out of the bathtub. "Aim a little higher, darling," Jo encouraged grimly. "Uncle Hal's mouth needs washing out with soap."

"Can't blame a man for trying," Hal teased. Tossing the keys she'd given him, he let himself out, still laughing.

"Future brother-in-law, my foot," Jo muttered, collecting wet bath toys. Jo had all but forgotten Mike, and he'd only been gone for two weeks. They'd met when Mike, in nearby Augusta for treatment on a bad knee, had visited Harriet over the holidays. They'd dated several times, and Jo, recognizing a fellow sufferer, had been perhaps too kind. The night before he'd left to go home he'd told her he loved her.

The trouble with being shy was that when you did open your mouth, there was no telling what would come out of it. How many times had she sat there and listened in horrified fascination to the lies that fell from her lips. "Oh, yes, the all-you-can-eat fried platter is one of my favorites," she'd said once when Mike had pulled out the dollars-off coupons he'd brought along on their dinner date. Actually, she found it revolting. "I've been wanting to see that movie," she'd confided on another occasion. She'd been the week before and walked out halfway through. It was as if someone else were pulling her strings. She *hated* herself when she acted that way, but she couldn't seem to help it.

Both babies were dried, diapered and in their pajamas when Jo heard the doorbell. She groaned. It had to be Mike. Harriet had mentioned that she was expecting him for a visit soon. Mike had bad knees, and there was a specialist in town who had had a lot of experience with the unpronounceable alignment problem that Mike suffered from.

"Oh, darn, darn, darn," Jo grumbled, raking back her hair on the way to the door. With Hal on a date and the others in Atlanta watching the Yellow Jackets play the Tar Heels, who else could it be? It wasn't as if she had dozens of friends who felt free to drop in uninvited.

"Don't either of you ladies move from that rug," she warned her two nieces. She glared at the lovebird, who always knew when she was irritated and tried to vocalize her into a better mood. "Ivan, put a cork in it, will you?" Then, reluctantly, she opened the door, wracking her brain for a valid excuse not to invite Mike inside.

But it wasn't Mike. Jo stared for what seemed an eternity, her thoughts tripping over themselves in an effort to reassemble. "Clay," she whispered finally.

His eyes were all over her, moving from her hair, which had come down during a wild tussle with her young charges, to the drenched shirt she wore over her jeans, to her face, which first colored and then paled so that every freckle stood out in relief. "Are you...all right?" he asked deeply.

Jo nodded. When the power of speech returned, she said rather sharply, "Of course I'm all right."

Shannon toddled to the door, beaming up like a sleepy-eyed cherub, and Chessie began to whimper. Chessie, small for her age and dark like her father, Pete, didn't care for strangers. Clay knelt and held out his arms to the two-year-old, and Jo swept up the howling three-year-old. They stared at each other for a moment longer, and then Clay stepped inside and closed the door behind him.

"There, darling, don't cry," Jo crooned, pacing and bouncing the child in her arms. "It's all right, it's all right, it's only Clay."

Clay allowed Shannon to explore his loosened tie, wincing when she discovered a tuft of hair at the open neck of his shirt and yanked on it. God, she's all right, he thought fervently. He didn't know what he'd expected, but when he'd finally worked up his nerve to call, only to have some strange man baldly announce the fact that she was with child!

Breathing as though he'd just run a fast uphill race, Clay let his eyes play over the tantalizing glimpses of her slender body revealed through the translucent wet shirt. Two things were pretty obvious—she wasn't wearing a bra. He grinned. If she'd had any idea what she looked like at this moment, she'd crawl under that hooked rug and not come out until the Fourth of July.

"Was that you who called earlier?" Jo asked. She spoke in a soothing monotone as she continued to walk. Chessie's eyes were beginning to close.

"Yeah. Who was the man?" Clay had shifted Shannon to his shoulder, where her head soon found a comfortable place in the curve of his neck. Jo envied her that with all her heart.

"My brother Hal. Sorry I couldn't come to the phone. I guess he told you I was bathing these water sprites."

"Uh, not exactly, but never mind." Brother, hmmm? Clay was inclined to be forgiving, under the circumstances. Hell, common sense had told him that the guy was off his rocker, but he'd reacted with a totally uncharacteristic emotionality instead of thinking things through. He'd slammed down the phone, jumped into his car, and blistered the pavement getting there. And been stopped by a patrolman for his troubles. His first speeding ticket in seventeen years.

"Hal came by to borrow my car. Ordinarily, he wouldn't be caught dead in my three-year-old sedan, but his wouldn't start and everyone else has gone to Atlanta."

Every time she reached the end of the room where the light from the floor lamp shone through her shirt, Clay felt his pulses leap. How could he be turned on by a bedraggled woman holding a sleeping child—while he was holding one, too? "Say, is there some place we could lay these two down? My coat's probably scratching her little cheek, and your arms must be getting tired."

Jo led the way to her bedroom, not wanting him there, but not knowing what else to do. She'd made a pallet of quilts and pillows in the corner. "Not the bed?" Clay whispered.

She shook her head, kneeling beside him to lower her burden. "It's hard to fall off the floor." She spread a light blanket over the sleeping children and then stood. Clay's arm came around her as if it were the most natural thing in the world, but it fell away almost as if her touch had burned him.

"Maybe you ought to grab a robe or something while you're here," he whispered. "Your shirt's a bit damp." Saint Clayton forswears voyeurism, he thought with a sigh of self-righteousness. But he'd come here to talk; he could do without distractions.

Jo collected a dry shirt from a drawer and lingered only long enough to change and clamp her hair back with a large barrette. By the time she returned to the living room, Clay was getting reacquainted with Ivan.

"I liked your hair the way it was."

"It's not my real hair, you understand," Jo said without a trace of a smile. "Actually, my own hair's short, straight and coal black. I happened to see this orange fright wig, and while I was trying it on, an evil genie appeared and waved his magic tube of superglue, and now I'm stuck."

Turning away from the lovebird's cage, Clay stared into the fathomless depths of her clear eyes for a long moment. "I knew that," he said quietly.

And then neither of them could think of a single thing to say. Jo began to collect the scattered toys, and Clay started on the picture books. When he'd located all five of them, he crossed to her desk and placed them beside the paper she'd left folded to the editorial page for the time when she could enjoy it in peace.

"What do you think of the Voegler Foundation? Will Harry buy it?"

It took her a moment to come up with an intelligent response; she'd been watching the way he moved, the easy play of lean, hard muscles under a civilized sheath of flannel and oxford cloth. "Hmm? What?"

Clay dismissed the topic with a murmur. He hadn't come here to talk about Harriet's self-interested activism, nor about the movement he'd got underway to turn the old Voegler place into a self-sustaining home for the retired. Seeing her against her own background, remembering the way she'd looked in his house and in her sister's house, it occurred to him that Joelle would have looked just right in any setting, in any century. In fact, when she was there, a house could be furnished in sackcloth and shipping crates and he'd never notice the difference.

"The foundation thing?" she asked belatedly. "I haven't read about it yet, I was waiting until I got the children to sleep." Helplessly, she allowed her hungry eyes to look their fill. It had been a week since she'd seen him; a week that had seemed more like a year.

Leaning his hips against the fake Queen Anne desk she'd rescued from a yard sale and refinished, Clay toyed with the cover of Aesop's Fables. "How've you been, Joelle? I've missed you."

Just before her strength deserted her completely, Jo dropped into a loose-limbed coil at one end of the sofa, her gaze still pinned to his dark, compelling features. "Fine, I've been just fine. I—I suppose you've been busy," she added hesitantly, and then could have bitten her tongue at the implication that she'd expected to hear from him.

"Yeah, pretty busy," Clay acknowledged. But not too busy, he added silently, to stop and wonder what you were doing at any given moment during the day, to wonder if you had trouble falling asleep nights, and if you were turning and twisting in your bed until the sheets felt like a straitjacket.

Jo watched him run a finger inside his collar. He acted as if it were too tight, but it had been loosened when he arrived, and Shannon had managed to undo another button. "Me too," she admitted. "Busy, that is. Harriet's decided to rid Greensport of pornography and vice."

"Here we go again," Clay groaned. With three strides, he was beside her. He sank down on the other end of the sofa and turned a grim look on her. "You're not to get involved, do you hear me?"

Jo's head came up as her spine stiffened. "I'm *what*?"

"Jo, I don't know what that woman's up to now, but I don't want you mixed up in it."

"Clay, I'm a secretary, not a . . . a suffragette. Besides, I don't see that it concerns you."

He hadn't meant to get the cart before the horse. He'd meant to take it slow and easy, but if she was about to get caught between the do-gooders and the porn shops, he couldn't wait for slow and easy. "Jo, do you *have* to work for that woman? Couldn't you find another job?"

"And have to go through all that hassle again? The interviews, the questions? Clay, have you ever been interviewed? They ask all sorts of personal questions, and if you hesitate, they look at you as if you were hiding some sort of criminal record."

He supposed being interviewed could be pretty traumatic, given her inhibitions, but all the same . . . "Do you *like* working for Harriet?"

She couldn't look him in the eye and give a truthful answer. Once more, her hesitation worked against her. Dismayed, she saw the quick narrowing of his eyes, the challenging set of his jaw.

"You hate it," he stated flatly.

"I—it's . . . not always what I . . . ah, expected."

"Banging on doors, demanding signatures?"

"Only three days of that," she defended.

"Delivering ultimata to newspaper editors?"

"That's because Harriet says secretaries always screen the mail, and . . . and the post office missends it, and—"

"Is that what you want to do with your life?" His eyes bored into hers, and Jo was aware of a small muscle just below his temple that clenched now and then, as though he were barely restraining himself from an act of violence.

She wrapped her arms around herself, wondering just how she came to be discussing her job with the likes of Clayton Abbott. "As long as I can stay behind the scenes, it's not so bad. At least it pays the rent. Birdseed doesn't grow on trees, you know," she said with a feeble attempt to lighten the atmosphere, which had quickly become oppressive.

"Surely you could find something more to your liking that would pay as well. I don't imagine Harriet's overly generous."

"Waitressing? Clerking in a store? I even thought about the newspaper office when I got out of business school, but after one look at the way everyone was jam-packed into the same big room, I couldn't get out of there fast enough." She laughed, remembering that day. So certain her newly certified skills would land her a glamorous, if behind-the-scenes job, on the *Greensport Daily*, she'd been ready to start at the bottom—quite literally. A cubbyhole in the basement would have suited her just fine, but not the madhouse she'd been shown after her interview. "Clay, I know it's crazy, but I can't help it. People make me nervous. I just freeze up and feel like an idiot, and because I feel so stupid, I do and say stupid things."

"You're talking to me. I haven't heard anything that leads me to believe you're a fool," he said quietly, reaching for the hand that had flown up to her teeth. "Don't do that, Jo."

She grimaced. She might not sound like one at the moment, but she felt like one. "You're... different. I've read your things ever since you took over the paper, and I—I felt as if I knew you," she admitted, drawn out by the strange power he seemed to exert over her, if no closer to understanding it.

"What about children? There's a new day-care center over on Third."

"I could never take money for just looking after babies," she dismissed.

He frowned. "What do you mean, not take money? Don't you get paid when you keep your sisters' children?"

"For looking after family? Certainly not." She sent him an indignant look before she remembered that he had no siblings. How could he be expected to understand about family? "Clay, you help your family for love, not money. Hal will refill my gas tank before he brings back my car, but that's different, and when either of my brothers comes over here to watch games on my TV, they bring their own drinks and snacks." And after they finish those, they clean out the refrigerator, she added, but not aloud.

Clay nodded thoughtfully as a picture began to form in his mind. "Generous of them. What do you do while they're watching games, darn their socks?"

"Gripe a lot, usually, but then, I'm not interested in games. Fran and Hal and Chip were all big stars in school, and Syb was a cheerleader. I was almost tall enough for basketball, but I was too uncoordinated."

"So why do they come here to watch the games?"

"With Hal, it's only when his roommate's got a girl-friend visiting, and with Chip, it's because he's so messy when he watches a game. He really gets into the spirit of things. By the time he leaves, my house looks like a stadium after the last game of the season. Chip's wife, Candy, won't stand for it."

"But you do. And afterward, you clean up the stadium and restock the pantry for the next game, right?" He pinned her with a knowing look, and Jo shrugged.

"So I'm a wimp. I never claimed to be Joan of Arc, did I?"

"Then do me a favor. Stop trying to act like Saint Joan and tell Harriet you're not going to get involved in this new crusade of hers, will you?"

Trapped by the deceptively gentle grip on her hand, Jo pleaded with her eyes, and then with her lips. "Clay, I can't. If she fires me, what will I do?"

"Go to your family for help?"

"You don't understand, Hal's just left school and started in business, and the others have mortgages and children and—"

Slowly, he nodded. "Oh, yeah, I understand. Everyone can use another doormat. If you turn yourself into a good enough doormat, your wonderful family might value you enough so that you can eventually begin to value yourself."

She flinched as though he'd struck her. "That's not true," she whispered, struggling to pull her hand free of his vise-like grip. "It's not! You don't understand anything."

"Don't I? I understand enough to know that you're still hiding behind a security blanket. In some ways, you're no more mature than those two babies in the next room, and until you face a few facts about yourself—"

"I won't listen! You don't know what you're talking about. I'm twenty-seven years old, and—"

"My God," Clay exclaimed softly, still gripping her hand in a way that kept her from escaping his intimidating nearness. "I'd thought twenty-five and then scaled it back a few years. Jo, where the hell have you been all this time? How long do you think you can go on hiding your head in the sand?"

She could feel the coldness creeping throughout her body, robbing her of color, stealing her strength. Her eyes burned dryly, for the hurt was too deep to be washed away by tears. "I haven't been hiding," she said with every vestige of pride she could salvage. "Mike likes me the way I am."

"Who the hell is Mike, another of your wonderful brothers?"

"My fiancé." Forgive me, Mike, but this is an emergency, she prayed silently.

Clay's look was openly skeptical. He lifted her hand, and Jo did her best to curl her fingers out of sight. "Where's the ring? Did you swallow it when you ran out of fingernails?"

"I hate you," she seethed, twisting away as he leaned closer. "You're cruel and—and vicious. I just wish I'd left Ivan's cage door open!" She felt the warm currents of his laughter flow over her averted face.

"That's more like it," he exclaimed softly, drawing her stiff form into his arms. "Much, much better, my bloodthirsty darling."

"I'm not your anything," Jo corrected him, but her brief rebellion lost much of its force when his arms slipped around her and he leaned back, pulling her across his chest. "Clay, you can't do this."

"Can't I?" His lips brushed against her hair where it sprang from her forehead, and she could almost feel his smile.

"I told you I'm engaged."

"I don't believe it." His hands continued to stroke her back, robbing her of the will to resist, and then they slipped under the loose tail of her shirt.

She tried to lift her head, only to have it clamped down with one of his large, hard hands. "Thanks a lot," she grumbled. "I suppose you think no man would ever want to marry me."

"Did I say that?"

"You implied it."

"The trouble with introverts is that they spend too much time reading between the lines and imagining all sorts of wicked things."

With one of his hands toying with the clasp that held her hair in check and the other one tracing the path of her spine from her nape to the waistband of her jeans, Jo was in no condition to argue her case. If she even had one. She turned her face into his throat, inhaling the scent of freshly laundered cotton, a subtle fragrance, and something that was purely personal and excitingly masculine. He'd scored a hit with the thing about her imagination. If he ever guessed the part he'd played in all those fantasies, she'd have to leave the country.

The clasp of her barrette came unfastened with an audible snick, and her hair, freshly washed and wild as honeysuckle, sprang to life about her head. "God, this is wonderful stuff," Clay murmured. "Why keep it all bound up?"

"You must be joking. Can you see me going out in public like this? Dogs bark when they see me with my hair loose. A few hundred years ago, they hanged women for less."

"You're bewitching, all right, but I think you've misunderstood just where the real danger lies." His hand came up to the back of her head, fingers twining into the tangle of fiery curls as he tilted her face for his kiss.

"Clay, please—" she protested at the last possible moment.

"A kiss, darling, that's all I want for now. One kiss." His voice was husky, the blue of his eyes rapidly lost to the darkening centers. His mouth brushed over hers, lingering in each corner, pressing into the softness of her full lower lip, but making no effort to go farther.

Jo's long body uncoiled, her legs stretching out as she clung to him, one arm around his neck, the other one burrowing between his hard hips and the soft cushions at his back. Her lips trembled, then parted involuntarily, and he groaned.

One kiss. The words burned themselves into her mind even as his tongue began its subtle invasion. Wild sensations rushed from her lips downward, setting off alarms along the way. By the time his hand found her breast, it was throbbing and peaked with need, and she lifted one shoulder to press herself into his palm.

"Oh, God, what have I let loose here?"

The words were spoken in a hoarse whisper as his lips left hers and moved over her face, kissing first one eye and then the other. He brushed kisses along her temple and buried another one in the sensitive hollow of her ear, making her gasp with acute pleasure.

Jo managed to work her fingers between the buttons of his shirt, but it wasn't enough. She desperately wanted to feel the rough surface of his chest against her bare flesh. A button gave way to her frantic assault, and she held the shirt open and lowered her face, brushing her lips against the wiry flat curls.

"Oh, sweetheart, don't do that!"

Startled, she twisted her face away, burying it in the sleeve of his shirt, but he refused to allow her to hide. Capturing her chin, he turned her to face him. "Open your eyes, Joelle."

Frantically, she shook her head. Why had she taken the initiative? What did she know? Now she'd offended him and embarrassed herself, and—

"Jo—honey, what's going on in that wild, wonderful head of yours? Are you really that innocent?"

"Innocent? *Me?* Gracious, no," she blurted, cringing inside as she tried to ignore the hard ridge on the lap that held her, and the swiftly diminishing tide of desire that had nearly swept her away.

Swearing softly under his breath, he found her hand and carried it to his chest. "Feel that. Don't you know what you're doing to me? Innocent or not, I don't think you're ready yet for what's happening to us, and I'm not sure I can handle it without a little cooperation."

"I haven't the faintest idea what you're talking about," she said grittily, overlapping the opened front of her shirt and clamping it in place with her free arm. Without an undignified struggle, she didn't see how she could extract the arm that was trapped behind Clay's body, and he seemed in no hurry to release her.

"I'm talking about the fact that you turn me on like a high-voltage switch, Miss Middleton. I'm talking about the fact that you're not experienced enough to go in for a fast, strictly physical affair. So what am I going to do with you?"

Feeling the hated rush of warmth steal over her face, Jo did her best to assume an air of nonchalance. "As I see it, you have two choices—you can either help me change my status, or you can insulate yourself against whatever it is about me that turns you on."

"Shall I tell you what I'd rather do?" His grin was lop-sided, but it had the effect of making Jo feel slightly more comfortable, nevertheless. If he could laugh about it, then it couldn't be all that bad.

"Am I going to find it shocking?" she ventured.

"I could put it in limerick form. No—better not. The way I'm feeling right now, a typical limerick would only make matters worse."

"A redheaded wimp, one fine day," Jo mused. "Met a newspaperman, name of Clay."

"The effect? Instantaneous! Combustion spontaneous," Clay put in, and giggling, Jo wracked her brain for a punch line. "One thing is certain," Clay said dryly. "Under the circumstances, we can't toss 'em in the hay."

"Fire hazard?"

"Five alarm, at least."

The limerick went unfinished, but at least the tension was defused. Clay shifted, allowing her to withdraw her right arm. It didn't help when he brushed her hands away and insisted on buttoning her shirt himself, but Jo allowed it. She would have allowed him to chop off her left foot if he'd asked. Was there anything more pathetic than a dyed-in-the-wool wimp in the throes of an infatuation? she asked herself hopelessly.

"So," Clay remarked as if they were continuing an interrupted conversation, "we'll just have to spend more time getting to know each other. You'll have to tell your, uh, fiancé, of course, that you have other interests."

"Oh, Mike," Jo mumbled. "He's Harriet's nephew, and he's an even worse social disaster than I am."

"Is that why you took up with him? You felt sorry for him?"

"Sort of. I guess. According to Harriet, he's always been too shy to ask a woman out, and the older he got, the worse it was. Imagine being thirty-nine and never having a real date."

"Thirty-nine?" Clay's eyes narrowed as he reevaluated the situation. The poor dolt might be perfectly harmless, but he didn't want her feeling too sorry for some frustrated, middle-aged guy who could take advantage of her good nature and her innocence.

"You see, Mike's mother was Harriet's sister. I expect they were a lot alike, so you can see how it could happen," Jo explained.

"Nevertheless, I don't think it's a good idea. If you've really let yourself be talked into getting engaged. How far will you go not to hurt his feelings?"

"Give me a little credit," Jo snapped, removing herself to the other end of the sofa.

"Credit has to be earned. Show me that you can stand up to Harriet and not get involved in any more of her harebrained schemes, and I'll—"

"You'll what? Let me marry Mike?"

Grinning, Clay stood up and began tucking his shirttail back into his pants. Jo averted her eyes. She hadn't realized how much damage she'd done. "I'm not that altruistic, but at least I'll help you get a little of the experience you so desperately lack.''

"Big-hearted Clayton."

"I've already done you one favor, whether or not you appreciate it," he said modestly. "You can talk in whole paragraphs without stammering or running for cover. That's a decided improvement, wouldn't you say?"

Jo threw a pillow at him, and Ivan jumped in excitedly with a shrill series of squawks.

"Stow it, Ivanhoe," Clay commanded. Crossing to the large cage, he lowered his head until his eyes were on a level with the tiny green and red lovebird. "You keep an eye on this wench and don't let her do anything dangerously stupid, do you hear me? If I find out she's been turning herself into a doormat again, you're going to wind up skewered between chunks of onion and pineapple, floating in barbecue sauce."

Six

Three days of temperatures in the low seventies brought green shoots burgeoning out of the wet earth. Forsythia cast off the gray bonds of winter and flung its golden bounty in all directions.

Joelle had her hair cut.

The last time she'd ventured into a salon, several years before, she'd been given a new operator who was even less sure of herself than Jo was. The results had been disastrous. This time she asked Fran for the name of her hairdresser and made an appointment for a styling and cut.

"It's glorious," the woman said. "If it was mine, I'd trim the split ends, thin it here and here to give it shape, and let it alone."

"Short," Jo said. She'd made up her mind, and she wasn't about to slink out with the job half done. Glancing around at the pictures showing the latest styles, it occurred to her that the "afters" looked more like the "befores" of a few years ago. "Nothing too extreme," she said warily. "I'd like it to look nice, but sort of...average."

The woman threw back her head and laughed and then set to work. With the first gritty bite of the scissors, Jo felt her courage drain away, but it was already too late. She closed her eyes and told herself that it would grow back. Meanwhile, she could always wear a sack over her head.

"Take a look, honey, see what you think."

Reluctantly, she opened her eyes and peered at the reflection of a redheaded stranger swaddled in a brown plastic cape. Experimentally, she tilted her head and then lifted a hand to touch the short, flyaway curls that danced about her face like a bright, shaggy helmet.

"Like it?"

"I—it's...different," she conceded.

"Sure is, honey. I got customers who'd sign their souls away to have hair like yours. If it's curly they want it straightened; if it's straight they want it curled. Color like that doesn't come in a bottle, either, not for any amount of money, and as for body..." She shook her head admiringly.

In the privacy of the dressing room, Jo stared at herself again, hardly believing the difference a decent cut could make. Why on earth had she waited so long to have it done? If it hadn't been for Clay, she'd probably never have found the courage, but he'd practically dared her to grow up.

Not that she equated having her hair cut with growing up. Still, it was a beginning, a long overdue first step. "Long *long* overdue! Here I am staring thirty in the face, and twice thirty is sixty, and twice sixty is a hundred and twenty, and—"

She hurriedly slipped into her blouse, seeing her whole life flash past before she'd even had a chance to live it. Mentally figuring the tip, she impulsively doubled it and then, not knowing how to handle the matter gracefully, pushed it at the cashier and mumbled, "For Lori—please."

By the time she got home again some two hours later, she was wavering between euphoria and sheer panic, stunned by the knowledge that she'd wiped out practically her entire savings. The saleswoman had insisted the turquoise had been created with her in mind, and the pale-blue sundress had looked so lovely on the mannequin. There was more, much more—shoes, silky underthings in colors she'd never dreamed of, and a flacon of the scent that was being promoted that month in the store.

On the way home, she'd salved her conscience by buying Ivan a quarter of a pound of cashews and a bunch of seedless grapes.

Carefully, she hung her new dresses in the closet beside the dark-green one that Sybil had picked out for her four years ago and the three or four outfits Fran had passed on. She'd never worn any of Fran's hand-me-downs, but her younger sister made such a production of giving her things, that Jo couldn't bring herself to hurt her feelings by rejecting them. Aside from different life-styles and different tastes, they had completely different body types. At five-five, Fran was nicely rounded in all the right places. At five feet nine, Jo had too much leg and not enough breast. Besides which, she lacked Fran's flair for the latest fashion. Jo's favorite style was camouflage.

Before she had quite recovered from the shock of what she'd done, Mike called. In no mood to deal with his awkward persistence, Jo tried to put him off. "I've had a hectic day," she claimed truthfully.

"Aunt Harriet said you had the whole afternoon off."

"Uh . . . yes, but—"

"Did she tell you I was being admitted for surgery in the morning?"

"Oh, Mike, your knees?" Mike's knees were his favorite topic of conversation, aside from his work as accountant for a small office supply firm in nearby Warrenton.

"They're going to do the right one first, and if that's a success, they'll do the left after I'm out of the cast. Joelle, I'd like to come by. There's something I need to say to you before I go under the knife."

Jo closed her eyes and prayed for patience, knowing full well that there was no way she could refuse him under the circumstances. After agreeing to see him for a few minutes, she cleared away the litter from her purchases, talking to Ivan as she worked. "I don't think I even like him very much, Ive. Why did I agree to let him come over? Is it because I'm a nice person, or because I'm a weak-kneed coward? Don't answer that."

The bird climbed the side of his cage and rattled the bell, indicating a strong desire to be released from bondage. "Oh, sure," Jo chided. "You're a big help. Ivanhoe Middleton and his free ear-piercing clinic. You'd love to sink your ruby little beak into that poor man's anatomy, wouldn't you?" She washed a grape, placed it between her teeth, and opening the cage door, lowered her face so that Ivan could take it from her. "Oh, you like this personal service? Huh! You call it personal service; I call it blackmail," she teased, stroking his bill with the tip of one finger. "If you ever learn to talk, you've got me where you want me, haven't you? You know where all the bodies are buried."

Mike arrived shortly after that, and feeling guilty, Jo went out of her way to be nice to him. To her chagrin, he didn't even notice her haircut. Of course, he was worried about going into the hospital. Mike was something of a hypochondriac.

"Joelle, I have something for you," he said after several stilted remarks regarding the weather and his aunt's new gutters.

"Yes, Mike?" *Get on with it, get on with it! My God, was I ever this tedious?*

He extended his short neck as though his collar were too tight, and Jo commiserated with him as a wash of unbecoming color flooded his features. Mike wasn't physically unattractive, he simply didn't appeal to her as a man. Or even as a friend. Digging one hand into the pocket of his gray rumpled suit coat, he produced a small box, and Jo felt a sudden tinge of uneasiness.

"I want you to have this. I mean, I want you to wear it. Will you please do that for me, Jo?" he pleaded earnestly, all the while struggling to open the small velvet box.

"Oh, Mike, please, I can't." Jo stepped back, embarrassed for him, for herself, and wondering how she could shut him up before he went any further.

"Jo, you're all I have. I can't talk to Aunt Harriet. She always hated my mother, and I don't have any other family to turn to. Please, I wouldn't ask it of you if I had anyone else."

"Mike, it's your knee, not open-heart surgery." Jo moved back another step, bumped into her bookcase and sidled away. Ivan chortled and rattled his door.

"Once they get you in that operating room, you can never tell what might happen. I had a friend once who went in for a hernia repair and—"

"All right, all *right*," she cried. The last thing she wanted was to hear a recital of Mike's friends' bodily ailments. He might not have very many friends, but when it came to boring details, Mike had a phenomenal memory. "All right, Mike," she said, resigned. "If it will make you feel any better, I'll wear your ring, but only until you're out of the operating room."

"Out of the hospital," he amended. "If you're my fiancée, that's like immediate family. You can visit me any time you want to instead of just an hour in the afternoon and an hour at night." His flushed face beaming, he reached for her hand and fumbled for a few moments in an attempt to shove the tiny diamond ring on her finger.

"Here, let me," she muttered, doing the job herself while she still had some skin left on her knuckles. It was a poor fit. "But remember, this doesn't mean we're engaged."

"I know that, Joelle, but it will make me feel ever so much more secure knowing you're out there in the waiting room while they've got me on the table. I'll be completely unconscious, you know. They're putting me under, because I couldn't bear the thought of seeing and hearing all the —"

"All right, Mike, you don't have to go into detail," Jo cried, feeling her stomach lurch.

He shook his head in doleful anticipation. "I knew you'd understand. Joelle, anything could happen to me. Dr. Corkell said he'd never seen a worse set of knees in all the years he'd been practicing, but as long as they know you're there, they won't dare try anything...experimental."

He left shortly after that, and Jo leaned against the door, emotionally spent. "My God, Ivan, was I ever that bad?" It was a good thing for her that Clay had come along and shaken her up before it was too late. Perhaps someday a woman would do the same for poor Mike. But it wouldn't be Joelle. It was all she could do to rescue herself.

Two days later, Clay took her out to dinner. Jo went through agonies between the time he called and the time he picked her up, trying on everything in her meagre wardrobe. The weather had turned cold again, and her new finery was much too springlike. Her hair, too short to pull back and anchor, responded to the dry heat in her apartment by becoming completely incorrigible, and she was exhausted from running back and forth between Harriet's house and the hospital carrying Mike the books, toiletries, and special pillow he requested.

She skipped lunch to have a professional manicure. A hundred times afterward she lifted her tiny, Windsor Rose fingernails to her lips, only to force them down again. "I will *not* bite my nails," she vowed. "I am an adult, and I refuse to indulge in such a childish habit."

Mike's tiny gold ring with the chip diamond winked mockingly at her, and she started to tug it off, then thought better of it. They weren't engaged; she'd made it plain that the moment Mike was out of the hospital, she was giving it back to him. Still, it had seemed so important to him that she wear it.

Jo wasn't really superstitious, but what if she took it off and then something happened to him? She'd never forgive herself. "Why can't he settle for a rabbit's foot, like any other sane and reasonable person?" she demanded of the lovebird who was showing off his favorite acrobatic routine and managing to keep one glasslike eye cocked her way at the same time.

Clay wasn't coming, she decided exactly one minute past the appointed hour. He'd changed his mind, and she didn't blame him one bit. Five minutes crept past, taking an eternity to do so, and she straightened cushions, fluffed her hair, flattened it again, and considered changing into her flannel slacks and a beige fisherman's smock.

"Ivan, stop staring at me like that! I am not a giant, redheaded cockatoo, dammit!" Then, hearing Clay's firm step just outside her door, she tugged at the four-year old green wool jersey, smoothed her hair one last time, only to have it spring up again, and rushed to let him in. .

"It's all you fault, so don't you dare say one word," she warned by way of greeting.

Clay stared at the red-faced Botticelli angel before him, wondering what he'd done that was so terrible. If he wasn't permitted to talk, then he might as well act. Shoving the door shut with one foot, he reached for her and drew her stiff body into his arms. There was only one way to shut a woman up when she was being irrational, and he proceeded to do it with utmost efficiency.

Off balance, Jo could only cling to him for support, but after the initial shock, support was the least of her concerns. Stunned to realize just how badly she'd missed him, she gave herself up to the moment, relaxing her lips as the tip of his tongue began a cautious survey of their outward contours. The freshly shaved texture of his face excited tremors that cascaded the length of her body. As his tongue deepened its bold exploration, she gasped, her lungs filling with the faint hint of cologne and the tantalizing scent of healthy masculine flesh.

Hunger invaded her body, rooting out the mere hunger for food. Swiftly, it filled her mind, her soul, until she was ravenous for a feast she could only imagine. Clay stroked her tongue with subtle mastery as his hand slipped over her back, moving the soft fabric of the loosely fitted dress over the silky slip she wore beneath it. The friction alone was enough to spark an explosion, and when his other hand found her breast, his thumb toying with the erect and sensitive peak, she sagged against him.

Clay's marauding lips moved from her mouth to her throat. His hand dropped below her waist, his palm warming the rounded softness of her bottom to press her against him. With the hard evidence of his desire between them, he groaned and moved her gently to and fro. "This isn't why I came here, Joelle," he said, knowing even as he spoke that the statement was only partially true. He'd thought of little else since he'd last seen her.

"I, ummm—we..." *Brilliant, Joelle!* Jo buried her face in his throat and struggled to regain control of her breathing. She was burning up, consumed by a need so strong that it transcended her wildest fantasies. "Clay?" she whispered.

"Yes, darling?" He was having his own troubles. Closing his eyes, Clay tried to imagine himself stepping under an icy shower. It didn't help much.

"Would you... kiss me again?"

"Oh, God, don't ask me to do that," he groaned.

Jo stiffened, mortified by what she took as a rebuff. "I was only joking," pride made her say. "Goodness, did you think I really meant it?"

With a sharp oath, he lifted her and carried her, long legs dangling, fists flailing, to the sofa. Dumping her unceremoniously, he followed her down, reaching out to grab her arms before she could connect. "My God, woman, a man can only take so much."

She stared stonily back at him, waiting for him to finish so that she could slink away and crawl under the bed and hide there until she grew moss on her north side. Perhaps by then she might forget that she'd made a fool of herself again.

Holding her at arms length, Clay drew in a deep, ragged breath. "Joelle, it isn't that I don't want to kiss you again. God, even you know better than that!" She cringed at the 'even you.' "What I want to do and what I intend to do are two different things. I learned self-discipline at an early age, sweetheart," he said more gently. "Times like this, I wish to hell I hadn't."

Grimly, she waited for him to get it over with. He'd have a ready explanation of why he didn't want to get involved. A man like Clay would let a woman down gently. In limerick form, probably.

She felt a rise of hysterical laughter threaten, and scowled, willing it away. *Here's to the gullible fools, who never quite learn all the rules. They always get burned, they never have learned, any lessons not taught in the schools.*

"You're not ready to be rushed into anything just yet, Jo. Let's be patient a little while longer. It'll be worth waiting for, I promise you."

Well done, she thought with bitter admiration. The man must have had a lot of practice in getting himself out of a tight corner. "I don't think I care to go out to dinner, after all," she said with an airy disdain that cost her dearly.

The dinner was wonderful, and Jo was admittedly starved. She devoured every bite before her, promptly forgetting whether it had been fish or fowl, soup or salad. When Clay put himself out to charm, no woman would stand up to him, least of all a woman who was head over heels in—infatuation.

He admired her short hair, sounding so sincere she felt almost pretty. He noticed her nail polish and tactfully refrained from mentioning it. They talked about birds, and she learned about the difficulty of sexing a breeding pair of African Grays.

"Mine were all surgically sexed. So far, all but one pair is delivering, but they're still pretty young. Some couples are late bloomers."

They discussed the operation of a small-town daily newspaper. "I came here originally as managing editor of the evening paper. It was on its last legs, and the morning one wasn't any too healthy. The publisher was desperate enough to give me a free hand, and I ended up consolidating the two editions about a year and a half ago. Since then, circulation has almost doubled and the advertising's done even better.''

Jo watched the flickering candlelight in his eyes until she felt in danger of drowning. Her gaze dropped to his hands, and that was even worse. ''Do managing editors usually write for the editorial page?''

''I guess you might say I'm a three-headed monster. I'm wearing about three hats at the moment, but as soon as I can lure the right people onto the staff, I'll have more time to concentrate on what I enjoy most. Now, I pinch hit wherever I'm needed.''

Jo had almost forgotten about the ring until they were back at her apartment. Hesitantly, she invited Clay in for coffee, and he refused, claiming an early appointment in Columbia. Absurdly disappointed, Jo attempted to slip past him and close the door, but he was too quick for her.

''I don't care for coffee,'' he pointed out. ''What I do want is a few answers. Care to explain that little gimcrack you're wearing on your fourth finger, left hand?'' He closed the door and leaned against it. ''Did you think it would serve the same purpose as a cross?''

''A cross?''

''I'm not a werewolf, honey. A wolf, maybe, but flashing that thing in my face isn't going to keep you safe.'' Suddenly, he grinned, and Jo promptly forgot the lesson she'd learned at his hands mere hours before. ''You're safe only as long as I can hang onto my better judgment, woman. I wouldn't push my luck, if I were you.''

''Who said I wanted to be kept safe?'' she retorted daringly.

Clay groaned. "Don't tempt me. And don't try to tell me you've suddenly got yourself engaged, because I won't believe it."

Jo looked down at her rosy fingernails, their brief perfection evidence of her determination to grow up and take control of her own life. "No, I don't suppose you would," she said quietly.

"And don't deliberately misread me, either." He waited for her to look up. When she didn't, he gripped her arms. "Joelle, dammit, look me in the eye and tell me what's going on. There's a limit to my patience!"

Flinging her head back, she forced herself to meet the narrowed intensity of those startlingly blue eyes. The intoxication that swept over her had little to do with the bottle of wine they'd split with dinner. "Really? What about that famous self-control of yours?"

His fingers bit into her arms, and she flinched. Instantly, he dropped his hands, looking contrite and angry and frustrated all at the same time, and Jo relented. "The ring belongs to Mike. Harriet's nephew, remember I told you about him?"

"So?"

"So... Mike's gone into the hospital for surgery and he asked me to—to wear this for him."

"Meaning?"

Jo frowned. "Meaning what?"

"That's what I want to know. Surely you don't consider yourself engaged to him. Or do you?" He frowned.

"Of course I don't," she said hastily. "I'm just sort of—well, like a security blanket."

Leaving the door, Clay crossed to the sofa and sprawled against the carefully arranged cushions. He covered his eyes with a hand, palm outward, and groaned. "A security blanket. God, that's even worse. You've done it again, haven't you? I thought you were coming along so well, and here you allow yourself to be *used* again."

Automatically Jo began to formulate excuses. "Oh, well, it's not really—I mean poor Mike doesn't have anyone but Harriet, and—"

"Enter little Jo, the perennial sacrificial virgin."

Ice crept along her veins even as the blood flamed in her face. "I wish you'd leave, Clayton. I was getting along perfectly well before you barged into my life, and I can do without your criticism of my—of my..." Her voice wobbled off into space, and she turned away abruptly.

He was on his feet, towering over her, in one powerful surge. "Before *who* barged into *whose* life?" he demanded softly. "One of these days, you're going to try my patience too far, Joelle."

And then he was gone.

The door had no sooner closed behind him than Jo was ready to call him back and apologize. What on earth had happened? One minute they'd been friends, the next he'd been hurling abuse at her, as though he considered the small favor she was doing for Mike a personal affront.

"I thought I was a mess, Ive," she said, her voice sounding as weak and watery as she felt. "I'm beginning to think I'm not the only one. Why should Clay care if I turn myself into a doormat for half of Greensport?"

At any other time in her life Jo would never have dreamed of getting involved in a demonstration, but by the following Tuesday she'd been reduced to a shapeless wad of putty in Harriet's manipulative hands. Ever since Clay had stalked out of her apartment she'd alternated between fits of determination and bouts of self-pity. She spent half her time berating herself for being such a wimp, the other half making excuses for agreeing to keep Fran's kids over the weekend, for lending Hal her car again, and for letting Harriet push her into joining the women's march against the All-Girl Staff.

She had yet to discover exactly what it was that the "girls" did behind those dark and windowless walls, having gotten no more than an indignant look from Harriet when she'd asked. At least she'd held her ground in one area; she would march for one hour only, and she refused to carry the sign accusing the city fathers of treading on the backs of innocent women. With her vivid imagination, she wouldn't be able to keep a straight face.

If only the rain had held off. With her tangled mat of hair darkening and dripping disconsolately down her neck, Jo told herself that at least no one would ever recognize her. She buried her chin in the collar of her beige trench coat and slogged along behind Mrs. Childress, the Sunday School Superintendent, carrying a limp cardboard sign that said simply, For Shame.

During the next forty-five minutes, two cars and a pickup truck pulled into the adult book store portion of what Harriet's group referred to as "that disgusting place." The men whistled, a couple of them applauded the bedraggled marchers, and one or two called out lewd suggestions. Jo buried her face deeper in her collar and waded through another puddle. She was drenched to the skin, but at least her hour was nearly up. She'd driven Harriet and three other women to the site in Harriet's car, which meant she'd have to walk home.

Seventeen more minutes. Sixteen, and then fifteen. She was numb from the knees down, aching from the knees up, and if the All-Girl Staff offered massages, she'd be first in line.

The flashing blue lights rounded the corner of River and First just as another car pulled up beside her. Jo halted uncertainly as placards fell to the ground and the wavering line began to break up.

"Hold your positions, ladies," Harriet barked shrilly. "Remember the—"

Whatever it was they were to remember Jo never knew. She was grabbed about the waist and thrown bodily into the car, the door slammed before she could even yank her raincoat clear. Seconds later they were roaring off down First Street, taking a corner on two wheels, the next one in a slightly less spectacular manner. Then, pushing the legal limit, they proceeded out MacLuckie Farm Road.

"Sit up and fasten your seat belt," Clay growled.

"It's a little late for that, isn't it? And I can't sit up. You slammed the door on my coat and now it's dragging on the highway and getting ruined!"

"Tough. Act like a child, and you'll be treated like one!"

"Oh? *Oh?* And I suppose you were acting like an ad—an adu—" Her nose tickled uncontrollably, and she sneezed. "An adult!" she finished as soon as she could speak again. "Who do you think you are, Clark Kent?"

"Believe me, I'm not feeling very mild mannered at the moment."

Jo sneezed twice more before Clay screeched to a halt in front of his front door and slammed out of the car. She managed to get her door open and was staring down at the ragged, muddy ruins of what had been a perfectly good raincoat. Good, that is, other than the fact that it no longer shed water.

"I hope you're satisfied," she said, holding up a filthy scrap of belt with a broken plastic buckle.

"Not by a long shot, lady, but the day's still young. Now come on and get yourself cleaned up and let's find out what the damages are."

Seven

With Clay muttering about lemmings who insisted on ritualistically hurling themselves off cliffs and Rudy alternately whistling and offering her a beer, Jo found herself being marched through the house, up the stairs, and into a large bedroom. She was dimly aware of nubby linen-covered walls, masculine oak furniture, and thick carpet in a mossy shade of green. Far too miserable to speak up in her own defense, she could only shiver and wait for the lecture to come to an end.

Which it did. Abruptly. "Bath's through there," Clay said gruffly. "Make it deep and hot, and stay in it until your teeth stop chattering."

"You didn't have to rescue me," Jo muttered resentfully, but he was already passing through the door. "You didn't have to bring me here," she called after him. The thought of the scene they'd left behind—the police cars closing in on all those poor, frightened women, brought a fresh bout of shivers, and she began peeling off her cold, wet clothing.

Not that any of them would actually go to jail. People like Harriet Brower didn't go to jail. Harriet had wanted to focus attention on a particular situation and she had succeeded. Jo had hesitantly suggested that perhaps a permit of some sort was required, but Harriet had argued that permits were for parades and septic tanks, not for demonstrations. And although Jo had been unconvinced, she hadn't had the courage to argue. Knowing how Harriet's mind worked, by tomorrow the whole disaster would be Jo's fault.

Clay's bathtub was enormous, the deep russet porcelain a gleaming invitation. She turned on both faucets and watched as steam billowed up to cloud the mirrored wall. The few personal items in evidence were neatly arranged, and thinking of her own haphazard ways, she grimaced. He probably squeezed the toothpaste tube from the end and put the cap back on after every use, too. Was there anything quite so intimidating as perfection?

She had carefully folded each of her sodden garments and placed them in a neat pile before it occurred to her that she had nothing at all to put on after her bath. One swift glance was enough to tell her that if he owned a bathrobe, it wasn't in the bathroom.

"There's such a thing as too much neatness," Jo grumbled. Reluctantly, she left the steamy warmth for the comparative chill of the bedroom. "All right, if I were Clay's bathrobe, where would I be?"

Her own was hanging on a nail behind her bathroom door, sleeves rolled up, sash trailing untidily. Not only that, a few faint stains she'd been unable to remove bore evidence of Ivan's habit of perching on her shoulders while she read or watched TV.

"Hanging neatly in the closet, of course. On a padded coat hanger." She tromped silently across the carpeted floor, hugging her resentment to her as if it were a shield. "With the sash neatly tied and the lapels neatly smoothed down, and not even one used tissue in the pocket," she added maliciously.

The closet was a walk-in, and the navy flannel robe hung on a wooden peg just inside the door. The sash dangled, but so evenly that neither end dragged the floor.

The draft struck her naked backside just as she reached for it. Startled, she clapped both hands over her bare bottom and then felt behind her for the doorknob.

Clay was too quick. "The wall safe is downstairs, and what little jewelry I own is in the top dresser drawer. I thought I told you to get a hot bath."

"I think I'm in enough hot water as it is, thanks," Jo whispered shakily.

With her feeble attempt at humor, some of the crackling tension seemed to dissipate, only to be replaced by tension of another sort. Jo yanked the robe off its peg and flung it around her like a cape. Clutching the edges together, she turned, face flaming.

"I was not snooping," she said with as much dignity as she could muster. "What was I supposed to wear? My same wet clothes? If you have a dryer—"

"Sorry. I remembered where my bathrobe was as soon as I got downstairs. My housekeeper has a thing about the birds, so she spends most of her time up here. Have you thawed out yet?" He continued to stare at her, eyes darkening until all she could see were rings of blue flame. "Jo? Your bath—"

With a yelp, she tried to slip past him, but he caught her arm. "My bath!" she cried, twisting away, and he stood there clutching the limp woolen garment, his gaze riveted to a pair of long, shapely legs that leapt across the bedroom and disappeared into the billows of steam that poured through the bathroom door. "I left it running!"

Robe trailing from his hand, Clay stood rooted to the spot. Nothing had changed, not a blessed thing. The woman had become an obsession with him. All he could think about was what it would be like to explore every delightful crevice of her mind, every delicious inch of her body.

He'd been out of his mind to bring her here. Why had he taken off like a bat out of hell the minute he heard about Harriet's picket line? Because he'd known damned well Jo would be mixed up in it, that's why. So why hadn't he simply delivered her back to her own apartment?

Clay laughed harshly. No mystery there. In all his years of experience with the opposite sex, he had never met a woman like Joelle.

The trouble was, she just wasn't ready. Not while she was constitutionally unable to say no.

Keep the kids, Jo?
Sure.
Borrow your car, Jo?
Certainly.
Wear my ring, Jo?
Of course!
March in my parade? Get yourself hauled off by the cops?
Yes, Miss Brower, if you say so, Miss Brower.

All right, dammit, so he wanted her to the point where he couldn't think straight, but it had to be her choice, too. She had to come to him of her own free will, an equal partner, confident enough to take him or leave him. Yet the possibility that she might turn him down flat brought on a feeling akin to panic.

Like a man going down for the third time, Clay turned toward the bathroom. She'd forgotten the robe. Maybe she hadn't been able to find the towels, either. "Jo?" If you need . . ." His voice faded and died.

Seeing her there, her wild, wet curls a perfect match for his bathtub, her skin glowing like Georgia marble through the water, and the submerged triangle of fire burning so brightly at the joining of her thighs—Clay completely lost his train of thought. Dear God, she was lovely. The bathrobe slithered from his nerveless fingers, and like a sleepwalker he found himself kneeling beside the bathtub.

Jo watched, her eyes widening warily. Somewhere along the way, her fantasy had gone awry. Where was the gentleness, the droll sense of humor, the lofty ideals that shone through every word he wrote? Those were the qualities that had attracted her long before she'd met the man. She'd been totally unprepared for his stunning masculine sexuality. It had knocked her off balance the first time she'd laid eyes on him.

There was no gentleness in evidence now, no laughter at all in those eyes that were devouring her as if she were a feast prepared for his delectation. He was all sinew and bone, rock and steel. He was fire incarnate, and he was consuming her in his flames.

Jo settled deeper into the water until she felt it lap at her bottom lip, her gaze never wavering from the flushed features before her. She watched helplessly as he unbuttoned his shirt, pulled it free of his pants, and stripped it off, flinging it carelessly aside.

Nervously, she licked at the moisture on her bottom lip. She was acutely conscious of the way his shoulder muscles bunched as his hands flexed on the rim of the tub. And his hands—the fingers square-tipped, well kept, lightly feathered with dark hair . . .

A shallow breath fluttered in her throat as she visualized them moving over her body.

Her distraught gaze shifted once more, only to be trapped by the two symmetrical swirls of dark hair on his broad chest. Nestled in each swirl was a tiny flat disc the size and color of a penny. In desperation, Jo closed her eyes tightly, as if by not seeing she could shut off her fevered thoughts and deny what was happening.

"Don't hide from me, Joelle," Clay said softly. Feeling his fingers rest briefly on her shoulder and then slide beneath the surface, she tried to edge away, but there was nowhere to go. She felt the currents rippling against her body as his hand moved beneath the water. When he touched only her hand, she felt a moment's sharp disappointment.

"Closing your eyes won't make me disappear." He brought her hand up to his chest, moving it back and forth over the firm, muscular flesh under the dark hair. Her breath caught in her throat and she watched as his gaze moved from her face down over her partially submerged breasts. Even as her own nipples responded to his simmering gaze, she felt his harden under the sensitive pad of her fingertips.

"Are you warm now? Let me help you," he whispered, his voice little more than a ragged sigh. He lifted her boneless body from the water, ignoring the water that cascaded to the floor.

"I'm getting you all wet," Jo protested breathlessly. Unable to meet his gaze, she ducked her head, and was astonished to see each beat of her heart echoed in the trembling of her breasts.

Swinging her up in his arms, Clay followed the course of a single bead of water as it trailed a crooked path down one gentle pink slope to form a quivering drop that hung suspended from the rosy tip. He lowered his head, and with a slow, sensuous swirl of his tongue, drank from her breast. Jo didn't even hear the whimper that emerged from her throat as she unconsciously lifted her breast closer to his lips.

With one of his arms beneath her back, the other under her knees, she was helpless against the marauding gaze that roved the rosy length of her body. Beyond embarrassment, beyond all rational thought, she could only cling to him, one arm around his neck, the other around his waist.

"The bedroom will be cold, but I'll wrap you in something warm," she heard him promise as he shouldered the door wider.

He wrapped her in something cool and soft, and peeling back the sheet, deposited her, cocoon and all, onto the bed. Huddled on her side, Jo wondered if there was a fire hazard involved. She heard the dry rasp of a zipper, the rustle of clothing, and then she felt the bed give beneath his weight. She ducked her head until only the top of her head was exposed, the coolness there in stark contrast to the heat that licked through her body.

"Jo, let me in."

Feeling the rush of air when he pulled back a flap of the duvet, she covered her face with her hands. As if that would help. The flames inside her had long since burned through her fragile resistance.

"Jo, don't be frightened. I won't ask anything of you that you don't want to give."

That was the problem; she wanted to give him *everything*. "I'm not frightened," she whispered as he gathered her into his arms, suffering her elbows in his chest.

"Just let me hold you, that's all. You don't even have to uncover your face if you can't stand to look at me." Her hands fell away then, as he'd known they would, and Clay found himself once more on the verge of drowning in those enormous gray-green eyes. Didn't she know how beautiful she was? Didn't she know what she was doing to him?

A slender arm snaked out of the covers and moved hesitantly up over his shoulder. Clay resisted the powerful urge to crush her to him, to feel her softness give way to his aching hardness. His mind burned with images of a flash of long graceful legs, a slender, supple back, hips whose subtle curves defied description. Her small, high breasts, their tips like dusky coral, brushed against his chest, and he inhaled deeply, increasing the pressure until he could stand it no longer.

"Jo, let me love you," he pleaded hoarsely, fondling the fragile bones of her shoulder with a desperation like nothing he'd ever felt before.

As if unable to help herself, she moved closer, slipping her hand up to brush her fingers through his hair. She lifted her face until her lips were only a breath away from his, and Clay edged his body closer, gently forcing her legs to give way until their bodies were pressed together from breast to knee. At the soft brush of her fleecy mound against his thigh, he groaned, his loins leaping in response.

Slow down, slow down! he cautioned himself, knowing full well that it was far too late for caution. Ravening hunger wrestled with the inbred restraint of a man who had always prided himself on his cool intellectual processes. And lost.

Clasping her head, Clay wove his fingers through the wild tangle of curls, exploring the shape of one small ear before moving down the delicate tendons at the sides of her throat. He curled his knuckles into the vulnerable hollows of her shoulders, loving the feel of her, the scent of her, the sweet, intoxicating taste of her.

He kissed her as if he could never get enough, and still he wasn't satisfied. When her tongue ventured timidly between his lips, he captured it, caressing it fiercely with his. One hand slid slowly down the satiny surface of her back, delighting in the quick intake of breath, her sudden stiffening as he found the most sensitive areas. She was incredibly responsive.

His palm closed over the cool firm flesh of her hips, and he pressed her to him, allowing her to feel the full weight of his desire. *Slow down, slow down,* he cautioned himself once more, but he might as well have commanded a river to run from the sea.

He was moving too fast, and he knew it. "Joelle, don't be afraid of me, please," he whispered.

"No, I—oh, please, Clay, I don't know..."

Her mouth was so close, so tempting. Aching almost unbearably, he tasted once more, dipping into the intoxicating depths, savoring the secret textures, until he could stand the sweet agony no longer. With a soft oath, he tore his mouth away from hers and fell over onto his back, flinging an arm across his eyes. The only sound to be heard other than the steady drumming of the rain outside was the rasping sound of two sets of laboring lungs breathing.

"Clay?" Jo ventured after a small eternity. "What happened?"

The word he used then was not one he could have used in print. "What happened?" he repeated, his voice raw. "Nothing, sweetheart, nothing at all."

"Please tell me. Was it something I did wrong?"

Expelling a shuddering sigh, he turned back to face her, and Jo was shocked at the raw emotion there. Pain? Anger? His features had suddenly grown harsh, the planes and angles oddly flattened, as if some alien being had somehow invaded the body of Clayton Abbott.

As swiftly and unexpectedly as the notion had arisen, it left her. Those were Clay's eyes—darker, narrower, but definitely Clay's. And that was Clay's mouth that was twisting into a parody of a smile.

He touched her face, his fingers lingering on a constellation of freckles that trailed across one cheek. "Jo—honey, it's just that I'd fully intended to give you more time. So what happens? At the first opportunity, I manufacture an excuse to get you into my bed, and I nearly—" He broke off, breathing a soft oath.

"Clay, you didn't manufacture any excuse," she told him. "You saved me from going to jail. Or at least from being taken to the police station and—and being fingerprinted and—with all those people." She shuddered.

With another sigh, one that held more than a little resignation, Clay drew her back into his arms. The flames that had threatened to blaze up out of control a moment before were now partially banked, but he was well aware that he and Jo weren't out of danger yet. The coals were still uncomfortably hot. "Jo, you know what I'm talking about. I came so close to taking you just now, and I'd never have forgiven myself."

Under the weightless warmth of the duvet, Jo snuggled closer. "But there's nothing to forgive. Clay, I'm twenty-seven years old. I don't suppose I could convince you that I know exactly what I'm doing, but—"

He grinned, brushing his lips along her hairline, where the first drying tendrils of her hair were beginning to spring up rebelliously. "Nope. Honey, just think about it. Less than an hour ago, you were marching in a demonstration. I know damned well you hated every minute of it, but you meekly agreed to go along with the rest of those—"

"But only for one hour. And I got to pick the sign I carried."

Ignoring her interruption, Clay went on. "You're wearing another man's engagement ring right now."

"But I explained about that," she protested. "You know I only said yes because—"

"Because you don't know how to say no," he finished for her. Dammit, even in the midst of an argument, his body had a one-track mind. Just being in the same room with her was a hazard, never mind being in the same bed.

"Joelle, when I make love to you, I—"

"Are you going to make love to me?" she asked eagerly. One of her feet began tentatively to stroke one of his.

"When I *do* make love to you," he stressed, "it won't be because you're grateful to me for some imagined rescue, or because you're still all charged up emotionally from—"

"But Clay, I'm not grateful! I mean, I—"

He cut through her protests. "And it damned well won't be because I want you and you don't know how to say no."

Her fingers twisted in the hair on his chest, inadvertently raking over a nipple. "Then you do still—want me?"

"Do you doubt it? I thought the evidence was pretty conclusive."

"Me, too," she whispered, seriously threatening his good intentions with a smile so sweet it hurt.

Groaning, he buried his face in her hair and rocked her tightly against him. "Jo, what am I going to do with you?" he asked despairingly.

"We've already settled that." Opening her mouth, she fitted her teeth over the curve of his shoulder, laving his satiny skin with her tongue. It could hardly be called a bite, and yet she was shocked by a sudden fierce hunger to know the taste of his body. All of his body!

As if he'd been hit by a bolt of lightning, Clay stiffened, and mortified by her newly discovered cannibalistic tendencies, Jo scrambled back until she encountered the icy shock of wet linen against her naked back. "I'm sorry—I d-don't know what came over—Clay, I didn't mean to—"

When he didn't reply, but continued to stare at her through eyes gone dark as a moonless night, she groaned, slowly pulling a corner of the sheet over her face, which dragged still more of the wet sheet across her backside. "I think I must have picked up a few bad habits from Ivan."

Clay began to chuckle. She felt it first, then heard the deep, musical sound, and relief poured over her. "Clay, I don't know how to tell you this, but—uh, your bed's wet. You could at least have given me time to dry off."

"It could have been a lot wetter." He indicated the sprinkler head on the ceiling, and Jo smiled. Then she began to laugh.

"Have you ever set it off?" she teased, and he propped himself up on one elbow and scowled down at her with mock severity.

"Don't ask personal questions."

"I've heard of throwing a bucket of cold water on—"

"Jo*elle!* And I thought you were such an innocent."

Stretching luxuriously under the slightly damp duvet, she crooked one arm beneath her head and smiled enigmatically. "Oh well, as to that, with five kids, we always had a few pets. Besides, I'm coming along pretty well, don't you think? Can you believe that just a few weeks ago I couldn't even speak to a stranger in complete sentences?"

"And now you're in bed with one?" Clay suggested.

"Yes. No. I—it's—Clay, you're not a stranger. Technically—I mean, physically..." She sighed heavily. "What I meant was that I've read every editorial you've written since you came to Greensport. I've even kept all your limericks," she added, determined to make a clean breast of it. The confession wasn't nearly as difficult as she'd expected, and afterward Jo felt a sense of relief. "I used to be in love with Sidney Harris, and then I fell for George Will, but when you came to Greensport and started writing for the evening paper..." She let it drop, having revealed far more than she'd intended to. "I only meant I admire your—uh—

style. I mean your ideas. As a writer, that is," she floundered. If he laughed, she'd kill him!

"Jo, I'm honored," Clay said quietly after a long moment of silence during which he fought down the desire to take her back into his arms. The truth was, he was knocked for a loop. For his precious shrinking violet to have felt such a thing was wonderful enough. But for her to have admitted it to him, that was the most encouraging sign yet.

She was getting there, he told himself, fighting against the urge to rush the process. One day very soon . . .

Fired! To have quit would have been one thing, but to have been fired was unbelievable. After seven years!

Still in a state of shock, Jo walked the eight blocks from Harriet's house to her own apartment, burdened under the accumulation of all those years in two large plastic bags. It was still raining. Hal had her car again, but at least her new raincoat shed water. It was lime-green plastic, and she found herself longing for the anonymity of her old beige twill.

Fired. What on earth was she going to do now? She'd been too shocked to fight back at the time, but somewhat to her surprise, Jo found herself wanting to do just that. She'd like to march right back there and tell Harriet Brower exactly what she thought of her and her worthy causes.

It had been Clay who had toppled the first domino in the matter of the Voegler house. Jo had been the last to learn that Harriet was the largest shareholder of the consortium that owned not only the Voegler house, but the overgrown vacant lots on each side of it and the row of run-down houses behind it. The houses facing on the next street had all been condemned some time ago, the Voegler house all that stood in the way of the whole block's being rezoned and sold to a commercial developer with a dubious reputation for quality.

Thanks to Clay's subtle pressure, there was now a movement underway to establish a foundation that would enable the tenants, many of whom were retired from the building trade, to do the actual work of renovating the old Victorian mansion under the guidance of the historical society.

Harriet, of course, had backed down, trying to pretend that that was what she'd had in mind all along. No wonder she'd been so ready to drop one cause for another. Philanthropy was one thing; playing politics for personal gain was quite another.

"Old hypocrite," Jo muttered, striding militantly through the dismal, late February rain. "A lady always does *this*—a lady *never* does that. Bah, bah, bah, you bleating old nanny goat."

Getting into the spirit of things, Jo seriously considered retracing her steps and demanding to be reinstated. She'd been given no notice, no severance pay, not even the courtesy of an excuse. At least not a valid one. Running away and leaving her employer to the tender mercies of the police didn't count, as Harriet had been well aware of the risks when she'd organized that embarrassing demonstration. In fact, Jo was beginning to think that things had gone precisely according to plan. How else could Harriet and her cohorts have gotten so much publicity?

By the time she reached her own apartment, Jo had decided that she was happy to be rid of Harriet. Her rent was paid for the next three weeks. Her appetite had never been a problem—she and Ivan could live quite well on boiled eggs, birdseed, and fresh vegetables. He might have to settle for peanuts instead of cashews, of course, but then, in a peanut-growing state, his exotic tastes had always been an embarrassment to her.

Naturally, Jo realized as she dug in her overloaded purse for her door key, she'd have to start looking for another job right away. There were still plenty to be found. Unfortunately, most of them entailed meeting the public. Maybe something in a basement somewhere, growing mushrooms...

"Good boy, good boy, have you missed me?" she crooned, crossing immediately to open Ivan's cage. He rewarded her by an intricate maneuver on the trapeze that entailed turning himself upside down and wrongside out, meanwhile never once losing eye contact. Righting himself, he accepted her applause with commendable dignity and allowed himself to step up on her finger.

After making herself a cup of tea, Jo glanced through the usual assortment of junk mail. She'd deliberately got her name on all sorts of mailing lists because getting nothing but a few modest utility bills year after year was depressing.

One envelope stood out from the rest. Not only the obvious quality of the stationery and the lack of a return address, but the fact that it was addressed to neither Occupant nor Current Resident.

Jo felt a tingle that began somewhere in the vicinity of her elbows and swiftly spread through her body as she ripped open the heavy white envelope.

The single sheet inside held five lines in a bold, compelling script. No signature. But then, none was needed. A slow smile spread over her face as she brought the page up to her face and inhaled, hoping to catch a hint of the light, crisp scent he wore.

"Idiot," she chided herself, and settled into a chair to read the limerick Clay had written her.

> There once was a bashful young dame,
> Whose hair was the color of flame.
> When caught in the buff

She covered her duff,
And ran away blushing in shame.

Laughing and at the same time, feeling an absurd desire to weep, she leaned her head back and closed her eyes. "Ah, Clay, is it any wonder I love you?" she whispered.

There. It was out. She'd admitted it—to herself, at least. She loved him. She was in love with him, as well, and that was a bonus, but she'd probably started loving him long before they'd ever met.

"Ivan, you're a lovebird, which makes you an expert, doesn't it? So tell me I'm not crazy. Tell me it's perfectly normal for a woman to meet a man and bingo! She's head over heels."

Swooping down from the bookshelf, the tiny scrap of brilliance settled on her arm and waddled pigeon-toed down toward the hand that held the letter. "Oh, no you don't, you scamp, you're not eating the only love letter I've ever had in my whole entire life. Come on, let's start supper."

By seven-thirty she'd read the verse a dozen times, as if to divine a deeper meaning, but if there was one, it escaped her. She tried to remember a book she'd once read on graphoanalysis, wondering what the loops and verticals in the strong handwriting indicated.

At a quarter of nine, she gave up and called him. "Clay? This is Joelle. You remember—hair of flame, blushes with shame?"

"It was a bad choice of words, but it was the only thing I could think of that would rhyme. Until after I'd mailed it," he added with a chuckle. "When, of course, I thought of scores of words. Game, tame, came..."

The sound of his voice was like music, like the deep notes of a pipe organ, like the wind over the marshes that bordered the river. Jo realized that she was beaming, and she made a serious effort toward sobriety.

"Jo? Are you all right? You didn't catch cold or anything, did you?"

Jo shook her head vigorously, growing warm all over again just remembering. Clay had scrambled eggs for both of them, and while her clothes had dried, he'd showed her his aviary. They'd talked mostly about birds, and reluctantly, she'd changed out of his robe and back into her own clothes. On the way home, he'd been quiet, almost distant. Jo had been puzzled, but she'd have died rather than ask what was wrong. He hadn't kissed her, nor had he mentioned seeing her again.

"No, I'm fine," she said brightly. "I never catch colds. I'm probably the wellest person you've ever met."

Silence hung between them, a palpable thing. Oh, why had she called? She'd never before called a man in her life, but she'd needed so desperately to hear his voice. Her palms grew damp and her knuckles whitened as she gripped the phone, unable to let go, unable to think of a single word to say.

"I got fired today," she blurted.

"You got *what*?"

"Harriet accused me of being disloyal. She said she'd never be able to trust me after I'd run out on her, so she...let me go."

It seemed as if she could hear the lines crackling between them. Then he said, "Jo? Look, stay put, I'll be right over."

Eight

Junk mail, birdseed, a dirty plate and a milky glass. Jo swept and gathered frantically and then dashed into the kitchen and crammed the few dishes and the pan in which she'd heated her dinner into the oven. She'd have to remember to take them out before she switched it on again. She dashed into the bedroom, stared at herself in the mirror, deploring her still unmanageable hair, her nondescript figure and her unexciting face, and then began frantically digging in her closet for something that would disguise them all.

"Uh-oh, Ivan," she muttered suddenly, dropping the new turquoise jersey and hurrying to shut him in his cage, remembering his unhealthy craving for male flesh.

She secured the cage door and made a hurried survey of the living room, spotting her new raincoat where she'd left it inside the door. She'd bought it on her way to work that morning, deliberately bypassing the more sedate shades. By the time she walked through the door a few hours later, it would have taken more than the bright splash of lime-green plastic to cheer her up.

It was too wet to put away, and when Clay arrived, she was still dithering over where to hide it. She opened the door, the wad of wet plastic crushed to her bosom. Clay looked from her face to the raincoat and back again.

One sooty brow twitched quizzically. "Going out?"

"Out? Oh, you mean— This is my raincoat," she said inanely. *Wonderful, Jo! And this is my chair, and these are my books, and this red thing with the Raggedy Anne friz all around it is my stupid face!*

Clay pointed to the Burberry draped over his arm and said modestly, "This is mine."

By the time she'd made them a pot of coffee, most of her composure had returned. Clay didn't press. For all that he'd come rushing over as if it were an emergency, he seemed content to relax and munch the animal crackers, which were all she could offer him to eat.

"What now?" he asked, extending his long legs under her pristine coffee table—pristine only because she'd hurriedly swept everything off its surface and into a shopping bag that was presently hanging behind the kitchen door.

Jo tore her gaze away from the tanned and capable hand that held his coffee cup. It led directly to a muscular forearm, which led up past a shapely bicep to the very shoulder upon which she'd nestled her head a short while ago. "Ahhh—hmmm," she observed, trying to sound thoughtful, sounding instead as if she were in danger of strangling.

"Want to talk about it?" Clay asked.

"*It?* Oh—my lost job. Not really. I'm trying to put it out of my mind."

"Then let's talk about your immediate future. Any prospects?"

"Prospects," Jo echoed, munching on the trunk of an elephant. "I—uh—haven't had a lot of time to look around. I mean, it only just happened. Today. This afternoon. And I had to stop at the market for milk."

He nodded gravely. "I see."

Clay fought down a surge of impatience. One step forward and two back. At this rate, he'd be too old to enjoy the spoils of victory when and if he ever won the right. Yesterday they'd progressed far beyond this stage—in fact he'd been afraid they'd progressed a little too far. Every instinct told him that if he took too much, too soon, he'd live to regret it. Wasn't it Erich Fromm who had said that men and women could achieve love only when they had realized themselves to the point where they could stand as whole persons? Which made this a textbook case. First he had to help her to stand alone. Only then could he afford to ask her to take the next step.

"I'm going to start looking first thing tomorrow," Jo was saying. "Or the next day. Or as soon as I screw up enough courage. I haven't even read the classifieds yet."

It was a perfect opening, Clay told himself; at least he'd know she was safe. Offering her a job at the newspaper certainly didn't constitute interfering in her affairs. "Joelle, it occurred to me that there might—"

The phone shrilled, and Ivan set up his usual clamor. Jo excused herself, dropped her cookie and stepped on it as she leaped to answer the phone. "Oh, Mike, it's you," she said flatly.

Clay listened unabashedly as he swept up the crumbs and brushed them onto a napkin. He selected a rabbit from the few cookies left and beheaded it with deft precision. Whatever he was whining about this time, it was plain to see that she wasn't really interested. Why the hell didn't she tell him to bug off?

"Mike, I'm sorry, I just couldn't ask Harriet. I—she—that is, I'm no longer working for her, and anyway, Hal still has my car. I could lend you my spare set, but it will be tomorrow before I can get them to you."

Clay's eyes narrowed. Had he thought she was learning to stand up for her rights? Whatever happened to all those old stereotypes? With hair like hers, she should be telling that jackass where to get off instead of apologizing for not being able to jump as fast as he wanted her to!

The moment she hung up, he demanded, "What did he want?"

By all rights, she should have told *him* where to get off, Clay admitted wryly. Instead, she said, "The hospital sheets are rough. They're making Mike's skin sore. He wants me to borrow a set from Harriet and—"

"The hell he does! And what's with your car?"

"My car? Oh. Hal's car leaks around the windshield and they can't seem to fix it. He doesn't like to take it out when it's raining because his leather seats get wet and the water seeps down through the stitching and it makes the stuffing smell musty."

"I don't believe this," Clay marveled softly. "You do without so that your brother can keep his upholstery dry? Does he pay your cab fare?"

Her silence was answer enough, and Clay's eyes grew as distant as an arctic sky. "I thought there was hope for you, Joelle, but I'm beginning to wonder."

Defensively, Jo tried to explain. "Hal's only twenty-four, and he has to drive almost to Augusta every day. What am I supposed to do, let him hitchhike?"

"You have other brothers and sisters. Why the hell can't they lend him something?"

"They just won't. At least, not since—well, anyway..." She sighed. "Look, Hal knows how long it took me to save up for my car, and he wouldn't take any risks with it. He promised me."

"Oh, my sainted aunt," Clay uttered tiredly. "You really do like being a martyr, don't you? You don't even want to change."

"That's not true!"

Clay stood and carefully replaced his cup on the coffee table. "No wonder you got yourself a lovebird," he said scathingly. "It's as close as you're ever likely to get to the real thing." With that, he let himself out.

During the next three days Jo applied for several jobs and was thankful when she wasn't called back on any of them. In desperation, she'd even tried for a job in the business office of Sharky's Seafood, thinking that at least she'd be isolated from the customers. Unfortunately, the office was just off the kitchen, and the kitchen was a madhouse. In the few minutes she was there she found herself in the middle of a wrangle between the chef and a market wholesaler and a fight between two waitresses who were accusing each other of stealing tips. She wouldn't have lasted a day.

All right, so she didn't like hassles. Who did? Did that mean that what Clay had accused her of was true? Had she unconsciously been making a bid for approval by ingratiating herself with her family?

No, of course not. Her family loved her, just as she loved them. If she wanted to lend Hal a car, that was her business. And why shouldn't she baby-sit whenever she got the chance? She enjoyed doing it. If Clay thought she was being used, then that was his problem.

Even so, perhaps it was time she made a few changes.

Jo waited until Hal had time to get home from work, but not so long that he'd have time to shower, change, and leave on a date. "Hal, I need my car. Have they plugged up your leak yet?"

"Uh, well, they found it, but fixing it's another matter. Gonna cost a bundle, too."

"Hal, I really need my car. Won't your insurance cover renting something until yours can be fixed?"

"You've got to be kidding," her brother scoffed. "The leak didn't come from the wreck. Besides, with all the points I've got against me, I practically have to send them a stamped, self-addressed envelope so they can mail me my bill."

"Get a bike."

"It's raining," he protested.

"Oh, is that what got me all wet when I was walking home? So get a bike with an umbrella."

"Well, would you listen to little Miss Muffet?" Hal marveled. "Who's been lacing your curds and whey with pepper sauce, Joellabella?"

Next she tackled Mike. She took a cab to the hospital, and without giving him time to get started on his own list of demands, made her speech, having memorized it beforehand. She'd planned to slip the ring off her finger, quietly place it on his bedside table, and leave with their respective dignities intact. Instead, the darned thing jammed on her knuckle and she had to borrow his bathroom and use liquid soap to get it off. She left nursing a scraped finger, while Mike complained that the soap had left a film on the diamond.

At least it was over, and jobless or not, Jo felt better than she had in ages. Emancipated, in fact. She was beginning to think that losing her job had been the best thing that had happened to her in years.

No, the second best thing. Meeting Clay had been the real turning point in her life.

Clay. He hadn't called, and there'd been no more editorials, much less any limericks. Three whole days of no contact at all and she was coming apart at the seams. At least a dozen times she reached for the phone to call him and lost her nerve. What could she have said? You were right, Clay, I'm a wimp? I *was* a wimp, but I'm taking lessons in backbone?

On the fourth day, there was another editorial in Clay's corner of the page. Reading it, Jo found her throat tightening with emotion. It could have been about garbage collection, and it would probably have had the same effect, but this time he had tackled a particularly sensitive social issue, one that was usually glossed over with euphemisms and platitudes.

"Listen to this, Ivan," she commanded, settling under the reading light. "'The indigent,'" she read. "'The street people. The juvenile delinquents. The unwed parents. We affix our label, using the pronouns, *Them* or *They*, to insulate us from direct contact with those less fortunate than ourselves.'" Jo's voice faded, but her eyes continued to scan the lines of the short editorial that spelled out the reasons why government agencies and organized charities were not enough. "'We can no longer afford the luxury of uninvolvement. There is an illness in our midst that cannot be cured by legislated benevolence. The statistics referred to on the front page of Monday's *Daily News* are more than numbers. They are people. They are our neighbors. Young and old, black and yellow and white, Protestant and Catholic, Democrat and Republican, they live among us. They have names. They once had dreams. They are our friends, and they desperately need our help.'"

Jo dropped the paper, feeling as if she'd run a marathon. Her chest felt heavy, and there was a definite thickness in her throat. If Clay had called and asked her to throw herself bodily into the war on poverty, hardship and disease, she would have flung herself into the fray without hesitation.

When he did call, it was to ask her to baby-sit with his parrots while he went to Atlanta on business. "Something's come up," he said over the phone. "If I move fast, I may be able to solve a couple of my problems at the paper at once. Can you help me out?"

"By looking after your parrots?"

"If you're still at liberty."

"Oh. Well…yes. Certainly I will." She tried to find words to tell him how his latest editorial had moved her, but after a few stammering attempts, gave it up.

"Wouldn't you like to hear the conditions first?" he asked dryly.

"Conditions?"

Clay's sigh was clearly audible, and Jo sank down onto the arm of a chair, wondering what she'd done wrong now. "Have you had any luck in finding work?" he asked.

"Not yet. I've gone through the best bets and the so-so's. Tomorrow I tackle the last hopes."

"If you could postpone the last hopes for a few days, I'd be much obliged. Rudy gets morose if he's left on his own for too long. I'd better warn you that he expects his appreciative audience to reward every performance with fresh fruit, raw vegetables, or a chicken drumstick—preferably fried."

Clay chuckled. Jo smiled. She was an appreciative audience, all right. Too appreciative for her own good.

"Did I tell you I have babies?" Clay asked. "My gray's have produced at least two new offspring, and they need to be closely watched. There aren't many people I'd trust to move into my house and take over the care of my birds."

* * *

That same night, Jo wandered about Clay's airy living room, feeling like an intruder in spite of all he'd done to make her comfortable. The refrigerator was stocked with enough to feed a small army; he'd shown her the freezer, the stereo, all the TV viewing equipment and given her the freedom of his library. He'd shown her to a handsome rock-and glass-walled bedroom that featured an antique bed and several handsome pieces of chinoiserie.

"The babies can stay in with their parents for another week before they need to come out, but listen to them several times a day, will you? As long as they sound all right, don't worry. As for Rudy, I've explained, and in case anything comes up that isn't covered on the list I've left, I'll give you a number where you can reach me."

He was dressed in gray flannel and tweed, with a maroon V-necked sweater and a matching tie. Jo thought he looked absolutely splendid. She had done her best to pay attention while he showed her the ropes, but it wasn't easy, not when all she could think of was the way he looked *without* all that flannel and tweed, the way his body had felt so warm and hard against hers.

Collecting a battered leather bag, he turned to the door. "There are a couple of books of limericks you might enjoy," he mentioned. "You said you liked limericks, didn't you?"

"Oh, yes," she said eagerly, and he laughed.

Dropping his bag, Clay took her face between his hands and smiled down into her eyes, and Jo's senses leaped at the unspoken promise he seemed to offer and then, for no discernible reason, retract. "Will you miss me, Joelle?"

She nodded, unable to speak as she watched his lips soften. His kiss was over before she could even put her arms around him. He stepped back and reached for his bag, leaving her with her arms dangling awkwardly, her disappointment embarrassingly plain to see.

Several times each day Jo perched on a grain bin in the aviary and watched the large hollow logs in which the grays raised their young. There were three of the logs, each contained in a cage some six feet tall that opened onto the outdoor flight so that the adult parrots could come and go at will.

Rudy's cage, a large wrought iron affair, was located in the greenhouse that opened into the kitchen. Thanks to an innovative use of glass, the greenhouse was visible from much of the rest of the house. Jo placed Ivan's cage at the other end, amidst a jungle of greenery. Ivan was openly jealous whenever she paid any attention to the African gray, and she spent an inordinate amount of time placating him.

There was plenty of time to read once she'd called all the family to tell them where she'd be staying. Chip was a little put out, for he'd counted on her to keep his Schnauzer over the weekend.

"Board him," Jo suggested.

"He won't eat at a kennel."

"He's too fat anyway."

"What the devil's got into you, Jo? Are you coming down with something?"

"Growing pains," she retorted.

"What's that supposed to mean?"

There was more in the same vein when she told Fran that she wouldn't be able to drive Petey to the dentist, but Jo shrugged it off. It was past time she weaned her family. Meanwhile, she still hadn't found herself a job.

Clay called each night. He had met with his publisher and hired a new advertising manager. "That'll take some pressure off, at least. I'm meeting my prospective news editor in a few minutes for dinner. If it doesn't pan out, I might see one more prospect in the morning, but then I'll be home. How's it going there? Any problems?"

"No problems. Babies cheeping loud and clear, all digestive systems 'go,' and Ivan and Rudy are outdoing each other showing off."

"How's the job situation?"

"I won't be working at Ludwig's Cleaners or at the library. Someone beat me to the library job, and as for Ludwig's, the less said, the better. I have another appointment tomorrow at two." She sighed, dreading it in advance.

"That bad, huh?" The note of amusement came through clearly, stinging her into a sharp reply.

"Did you ask your new advertising manager a lot of embarrassing questions that had nothing at all to do with the job?"

After a moment, Clay asked, "What sort of questions?" And when she remained silent, he repeated, "What questions, Jo? Who asked them?"

"It doesn't matter. I wouldn't work there if he paid me five times that much."

Clay hung up, staring thoughtfully down at the drink in his hand. It was probably perfectly innocent. With someone like Joelle, having a stranger ask her age and marital status could be an ordeal. Somehow, he had an idea it had been more than that this time. He tossed back his whisky, swore softly, and wished to hell he was there, instead of here in a hotel in the middle of town with another woman waiting downstairs for him. Just hearing Jo's voice on the phone had got him all stirred up. Unfortunately, he didn't even have time for a cold shower.

In horrified fascination, Jo read limerick after limerick, each one raunchier than the last. No wonder Clay had given her a *look* when she'd told him how much she enjoyed them. Surely he didn't think—she hadn't *dreamed* that . . .

Great Scott, these were dreadful!

On the other hand, most of them were so funny she couldn't help laughing. A few of them were even clean. Had Clay read the one about the girl who wore the newspaper dress to a ball, where it caught fire and burned her entire, front page, sports section and all? Or the one about Titian and his model? Or the one about . . .

Yawning widely, she let the book fall shut in her lap.

What had awakened her? Cold feet, cricky neck, or just the sense that someone was staring at her? Slowly, Jo opened one eye. Quickly, she shut it again, half convinced she was still dreaming.

"I didn't mean to startle you," Clay said quietly. He was sitting across from her, his dark hair rumpled, his shirt awry, and his tie dangling from a knot halfway down his chest. He looked exhausted.

"I wasn't expecting you tonight," Jo said, her voice husky with sleep. The book over which she'd fallen asleep fell to the floor with a thud, and Clay picked it up. He glanced at the cover, and then back at her, a slow smile lifting some of the tired lines from his face.

"Find any new ones in here?" he asked.

Jo groaned. He would have to catch her reading the damned thing. What could she say? "Would you believe it just flew off the shelf and landed on the floor beside my chair?"

Still grinning, he shook his head. "Try again."

"Clay, they're awful! Is that sort of thing . . . legal?"

"Oh, it's legal enough. Been around since the days of Pompeii, at least. For a period of about five years, sometime during the late nineteenth century, I believe, there were actually a few clean ones written, but they couldn't hold a candle to the traditional type."

Having read several verses that involved innovative uses of candles, as well as various vegetables, Jo flushed and began busily searching for the shoes she'd slipped off earlier. "You're back," she mumbled. "I mean tonight. What I meant was, I wasn't expecting you until . . . what time is it, anyway?"

Standing, Clay stretched and extended a hand to her. Free will having abdicated the moment she'd awakened to find him staring at her, Jo allowed him to pull her to her feet.

He drew her directly into his arms, and boneless, she allowed herself to melt against him. "It's a quarter past two, and I've missed you," he said in a gravelly whisper. Jo, her face buried in the scratchy tweed of his jacket, didn't even attempt to speak. Either her tongue would have stuck to the roof of her mouth, or she'd have blurted out something entirely too revealing.

"Hungry?" he inquired softly.

"Just sleepy," she replied, and he turned toward the stairs, snapping out lights without releasing her.

"Birds settled down for the night?"

"Mmmm-hmmm." Lassitude was being replaced by a simmering sort of excitement as Jo took the first step, still held fast to his side. The pressure of his hip against hers was enough to rob her of all reason, and for once, she didn't care. Clay was back and she loved him, and he *must* feel something for her, as unlikely as that was.

At the head of the stairs, Clay turned. Holding her at arms length, he stared into her eyes until she felt something inside herself begin to flow out to meet him. "Have you been sleeping all right?" he asked deeply.

Was it her imagination, or was he having trouble with his breathing? "Yes. That is, no. Sometimes," she finished a little desperately. What did he want her to do? Confess that she'd disdained the use of the guest room and then lain awake the first night in *his* bed, imagining what it would be like to belong there—to belong to him?

Clay was speaking, but she hadn't the foggiest notion what he was talking about. She watched his lips form words, listened to the rough sweet cadence of his voice, and pleaded silently for him not to ban her to another night of restless, solitary dreams.

Almost as if it hurt him to do it, Clay caught her to him, groaning under his breath. "Ah, God, I tried!" The door to his room stood open. Sweeping her up into his arms, he stepped through the door, and then he carefully lowered her beside the bed until her feet touched the carpeted floor. Like twin rings of blue fire, his eyes burned into her consciousness with an unspoken question.

"Yes, oh yes, please," Jo whispered, standing on tiptoe to reach his lips. She could feel him shudder, feel the quick hardening of muscles and sinew, but he allowed her to take the initiative. Eagerly, if inexpertly, she kissed him, drawing the tip of her tongue daringly over the curving line of his lips. Her arms reached around him and she held him fiercely, desperately needing to be closer. Was there a graceful way to ask a man to remove his clothes?

Clay made no move even to take off his coat. He wasn't going to help her. Dismayed, Jo wondered if he'd suddenly lost interest. Or worse, if she'd misread his intent. If he was too exhausted to undress, perhaps he was too exhausted to...

But she could hear the ragged edge of his breathing, could see the unnatural flush on his angular face. Still, what did *she* know. Maybe he was only trying to hang on to his patience until she left so that he could turn in.

"Clay?" Jo whispered his name tentatively, slipping her arms under his jacket. At the feel of his hot, rigid body under her palms, a surge of excitement splintered through her, weakening her until she thought her knees were going to buckle.

"Hmmm?" he murmured. His arms were still held rigidly at his sides, but she could see the rapid, irregular rise and fall of his chest, feel it under her cheek. Heavy breathing wasn't a symptom of exhaustion, was it? Yet he'd made no move to kiss her. Or even hold her. It was as if he were waiting for something.

Was there some ritual she didn't know about? Some secret signal known only to the initiated?

Jo steeled herself to pull away. It was embarrassingly obvious that she'd mistaken his kiss for something else. He didn't want her after all. "I-I guess I'd better say goodnight," she mumbled, burying the words in his throat.

"Ah, Jo...precious, I'm too tired to be rational tonight."

He came alive then. Holding her in a viselike grip, he began kissing her lips, her eyelids, her nose. He came back to her mouth, and his tongue claimed a victory that was purely masculine, totally sensual. His hands raked over her back, pressing her breasts against the hard wall of his chest, fitting her pelvic softness against the aggressive thrust of his desire.

Without ever quite releasing her, he struggled to work one arm from the sleeve of his coat, and then the other. That done, he ran his hands under her sweater and quickly stripped it off over her head. "Let me look at you," he said unevenly, his gaze coursing hotly down her trembling body.

Half-eager, half-embarrassed, Jo waited, never more conscious of the smallness of her breasts under the wisps of sheer nylon that covered them. Why couldn't she have been wearing something more attractive than her old black corduroys? And socks! What good did it do to wear seductive tea-rose lingerie with thick white sweat socks?

With slow deliberation, he reached out and unsnapped the front fly of her pants. While she held her breath, he slowly lowered the zipper to its bottom limit, not releasing the tab immediately. She felt his fingertips slide between her thighs. Curving into the melting core of her femininity, his trembling fingertips seared her with a heat so intense that she nearly lost consciousness.

"Help me, Jo," he rasped, his voice harsh with need. Swiftly, he slid her pants over her hips, and then he captured her hands. Uncurling her fingers, he placed them on his chest. "First the shirt," he instructed softly.

She was trembling so hard she couldn't manage to undo more than a few buttons. When it came to unknotting his tie, she was lost. The tiny rims of newly grown fingernails inadvertently scraped over one of his nipples, and he shuddered. With a low groan, he took over the job himself, making short work of it. First the tie, then the shirt, and then, under Jo's fascinated gaze, his pants.

The dark briefs he wore underneath concealed, but they could hardly disguise the state of his arousal. Jo swallowed hard. She felt the swift rise of heat burn her cheeks, and she stared, unable to look away.

"Don't be frightened, darling," Clay murmured, drawing her into his arms again. "I'll never hurt you, no matter what."

"I'm not afraid," she said quickly. "Not really."

His mouth was moving over the edge of her jaw, finding the sensitive hollow under her ear, while his hands slid under the straps of her bra and moved them down her shoulders. "I'll do my best to make it last a long, long time, love," he promised, burying kisses in the vulnerable place where her neck joined her shoulder. "I want it to be so perfect for you, but—"

She writhed against him and felt the immediate response of his thrusting masculinity. She was burning, her thighs trembling as she pressed herself against him. "Teach me! Tell me what do do," she pleaded.

Clay lowered her to the bed and followed her down. He lifted one of her legs until he could kiss the back of her knee, and she gasped, shocked at the spear of pleasure that shot upward when he touched a small dimple with the tip of his tongue. And then he peeled off her long, fuzzy white sock, following the revealed tender flesh with a series of lingering kisses until she was all but helpless.

"Give me your hands, love," he commanded when he'd relieved her of all but the single scrap of nylon and lace about her hips. Blindly, she complied, and he placed them on his chest. "I need your touch," he said unevenly. "Could you . . . touch me and kiss me—the way I want to touch and kiss you?"

Jo moaned, moving restlessly against him. Her palms explored the sensuous textures of his chest, the wiry hairs that swirled and then arrowed downward to disappear into the navy briefs. She could feel the thunder of his heartbeats under the heated surface of his skin, the resilience of his musculature and the velvety softness that surrounded the erect pinpoints of his hardened nipples. "Yes, yes...oh, yes, Clay."

Her hands were everywhere, rounding his shoulders, stealing into the hidden warmth beneath his arms, venturing downward and then darting back up again to safer ground.

He cupped her breast and then circled the hardened pink nub with his tongue, driving her frantic. His hands slipped down to stroke the satin hollows of her waist, curving over the delicate bones of her hips. He buried his face in the softness of her abdomen, and when she felt his hot tongue flicker in the dimple of her navel, she cried out, her whole body stiffening involuntarily. "Please—Clay!" she whimpered. "Oh, please..."

"I want to see all of you, Joelle. I want to taste your honey and feel the sweet fire of you all around me." With a deft movement, he stripped off her pants, and then removed his own, never leaving her without his touch. His thigh against hers, his hand on her hip. And then he was kissing her again, his tongue making sensual promises as his hands played an accompaniment over her body, lighting the way for pleasures to come.

Light spilled in from the hallway, and Jo watched him, her mouth dry with excitement. She loved the raven darkness of his hair against her breast—against the flat plain of her stomach. She shivered when his thigh moved against her side, the soft hair brushing her sensitive skin. Curling her body around him in a movement that was purely instinctive, she raked his flesh with her teeth. The faint scent of soap clung to his body, but his taste was of something far more intoxicating.

"Yes, love, oh yes." Clay's sibilant whisper spurred her daring, but as she felt the tremors shake his hard frame, she drew back.

Clay planted fevered kisses in the vulnerable hollows of her body—at the base of her throat, the valley between her breasts. With a low groan, he moved up over her. Once more he found her mouth, even as his hands settled over the tangle of silk at the joining of her thighs.

Rhythms. The mating of tongues, eagerly seeking, darting and thrusting, tenderly circling and stroking. Rhythms that rocked her body, threatening the whole universe, until she could only hang on and gasp his name over and over.

Thighs trembling, she lifted her hips, blindly seeking that most intimate embrace of all. "Please, please, Clay—I can't bear it," she pleaded.

With unsteady hands, he stroked her hips, lifting them even more as he lowered himself into the cradle of her body. "Oh, love," she heard him whisper, and she drew the words inside her to savor, once this wild storm had receded.

It was Clay who held back, Clay who shuddered with the force of restraint as he moved against her blossoming womanhood until she was burning out of control. At the last possible moment, he thrust forward, broaching her with infinite gentleness. He captured her startled cry with his mouth, treasuring her in his arms as he waited for her to adjust to his masculine invasion.

Then he began to move. Slowly at first—tentatively, stroking sword against sheath until the heat grew too intense to control—and he was burning up!

He saw her eyes widen in surprise, darken suddenly, and then he felt her shuddering release. Holding her tightly, he leaped for the moon and the rapture broke over them, bathing them both in its glory. He heard his name on her lips, like a wondering prayer, and that was the last thing he knew before sleep claimed him, a heavy sleep that was filled with fevered dreams.

Nine

Jo must have slept. The room was warm with the lemony sunshine of late winter when she opened her eyes. At first she was only mildly disoriented. Then, as the events of the past few hours began to return, panic set in.

Close by, someone was breathing heavily. Not snoring, but breathing with a depth and slowness that indicated deep sleep. Without moving her head, she cast a sidelong glance. Clay was sprawled on his stomach, a pillow covering the top of his dark and tousled head. His face was turned toward her, and Jo marveled at the textural contrast between his long, silky lashes and the shadowy bristles that darkened his jaw. Both arms were flung against the headboard, bunching the muscles of his massive shoulders.

Her gaze swept down the length of the king-size bed. Either Clay had thrown off the covers or she'd hogged them all. He was totally bare from the thighs up.

Mesmerized, Jo stared at the unexpected scattering of freckles across his tanned back. Under a dusting of black hairs, his legs were tanned as well. Her gaze was drawn magnetically to his firm, small buttocks, the paleness of which clearly revealed the cut of his trunks.

In February? He hadn't got that tan in Greensport, Georgia.

Dear Lord, what did she know about this man? Nothing! Absolutely nothing, and she'd given herself to him in the most intimate way of all.

Given! She'd practically *forced* herself on him.

Stealthily, Jo eased one leg off the edge of the bed, following it with the other. An assortment of aches and stiffnesses hit her at once, bringing back vivid memories of the night just past. She stood, careful not to rouse the man beside her. Her clothes were scattered about the floor, the rest of her things down the hall in the guest room. With any luck, she could make it out of here before he caught her.

Out of the house and, if possible, out of the country.

On her knees at the foot of the bed searching for her other sock, she heard the soft jangle of the phone. Her heart slammed into her tonsils, and she froze, ready to scramble under the bed and wait it out.

Clay's prone body happened to be at her eye level. Warily, Jo watched him as he muttered something in his sleep and flopped one arm down at his side. When the phone rang again, she held her breath, certain that this time he'd wake up.

He didn't. Either Clay was an unusually heavy sleeper or he was totally exhausted. Or both.

It came a third time, the oddly muted buzz. Jo wondered if she should smother the blasted thing under a pillow or disconnect by lifting the receiver and replacing it. But if she did that, whoever was calling would probably redial. Clay might be able to sleep through anything, but by now Jo's shredded nerves were raw.

Sock forgotten, she crawled across the floor, still on her knees, and let herself out, getting to her feet again only when she was safely on the other side of the bedroom door. At least the ringing had stopped. In the process of expelling a sigh of relief, she heard it start again, a decidedly unmuted summons from the room at the other end of the hall. The sigh turned into a soft oath of exasperation and, clutching her clothes, Jo dashed to answer the thing before Clay woke up.

She was in no condition to deal with him. Not yet. Her whole world had been knocked out of its safe little orbit, and she needed time to think. Six months or a year. Maybe five years would do it.

There'd been a time when Jo had prided herself on the clarity of her thought processes. With all her faults, she'd never actually doubted her own intelligence. The trouble came only when she tried to verbalize those thoughts. Then she'd met Clay and something had happened to her. She began speaking in whole paragraphs.

But that was before. Now, after last night, she wondered if she'd ever be coherent again.

Locating the phone between an atlas and a stack of almanacs in the room that seemed to be part study, part bedroom, she snatched it up, a "call back later" message already taking shape in her mind.

"Clay?" a woman's voice asked.

"Asleep," Jo said tersely. "C-could you call—"

A knowing chuckle on the other end froze her midmessage. A woman's husky contralto said, "I don't wonder, after these past few nights. Look, this is Theresa Leinbach. Give him a message for me, will you? Tell him he was in such an almighty hurry last night that he left his coat here.

I'll be down on Friday, but if he needs it before then, he can give me a call and I'll express it to him. If not, I'll bring it with me.''

Feeling as if she'd just been kicked in the stomach, Jo clutched the phone until her fingertips whitened. "Yes. I mean, I'll leave a message. Is—is that all?''

"All for now, at least.'' She sounded as if she were amused. "Who are you? Housekeeper? Secretary? Lady friend?''

Jo hung up without answering. Like a sleepwalker, she returned to the guest room and began gathering up her things. Within minutes she was on her way downstairs, clutching her overnight bag. She heard Clay call her name just as she located her purse, and without answering, she dashed out the front door, tossed the bag into the back seat and took off, not even waiting to fasten her seat belt. There were dangers, and then there were . . . *dangers*!

Her body ached in the most unlikely places, but Jo closed her mind to that. She closed her mind to all but the desperate need to run.

Never in her whole life had she been so close to another human being. For one brief moment, she'd truly been a part of him, not only physically, though that had been shattering enough—but mentally, spiritually, emotionally. She'd never felt so . . . *threatened* in her entire life!

A hundred years from now, perhaps she'd be able to look back on what had happened and smile, but for now, she only knew she had to get away.

Halfway home, she remembered Ivan. Dear Lord, couldn't she ever do anything right? What now, go back and pound on the door and ask for her bird? *Hi there, Clay!* she could hear herself saying. *Making love with you was absolutely the most momentous, earth-shaking event in my en-*

tire twenty-seven years—oh, and by the way, I forgot my bird.

Clay would really get a kick out of that, wouldn't he? If he hadn't gone back to bed. It occurred to Jo that she'd forgotten to give him the message from Theresa Leinbach, and she didn't care. She'd always hated women with low, sexy voices. They threw you off guard by sounding so damned friendly.

No wonder Clay had been exhausted. Old Theresa had been so *friendly* to him he couldn't even remember to collect his clothes!

Jo's eyes began to sting, and she blinked angrily. She wasn't a crier. She certainly wasn't going to shed tears just because she'd slept with a man and been awakened by the women he'd just left. It wasn't the end of the world.

It only seemed that way.

Her phone was ringing when she let herself into her own apartment. She was tempted to let the blasted thing ring. She wasn't in the mood for any more phone calls. But it might be one of her family. Guiltily averting her eyes from Ivan's empty cage, she dropped her suitcase and lifted the receiver.

"Joelle? What the hell got into you? Didn't you hear me calling you? What made you—"

Slowly she replaced the phone, and then she lifted it from the cradle again. At the sound of the buzzing dial tone, she slid the whole thing under a sofa cushion. Then she sank down into a chair, staring blindly at the drooping white blossoms of a shamrock plant. She should have watered it before she'd left. Maybe she'd have had better luck.

Half-formed questions drifted into her consciousness and out again, unanswered. Whose idea had it been, making love? Had she actually taken the initiative? Had she only imagined his reluctance? She hadn't imagined him just standing there, arms hanging at his sides, while she kissed him and stroked him and all but begged him to take her.

Oh, dear Lord, she'd never done anything so shameless in her life! He'd be laughing at her from now on.

Who *was* Theresa Leinbach? Why would he have left his coat with her unless—?

"Well, that's pretty obvious, you ninny. Business trip, indeed. No wonder he was so tired. No wonder you practically had to force him to make love to you." Finding no solace in moping, she jumped up and turned to Ivan's cage. Oh, shoot, she'd forgotten!

At least she could do something about her poor neglected plants. Her cactus was leaning, and she poked between the spikes with a forefinger and then rearranged the rocks around its base. Turning to the drooping shamrock, she murmured, "I don't blame you for not wanting to look me in the eye. I'll get you some warm water, you just wait right here."

A moment later, gathering the cloverlike leaves in one hand, she held them up while she carefully watered the soil. "Sorry, Maureen. I wouldn't blame you if you sent me a month of bad luck. I'll get you a fresh fertilizer stick the next time I go to the—"

A new and terrifying thought occurred. What if she were pregnant? She was pretty sure Clay hadn't taken any precautions, and goodness knows, she hadn't been prepared. She'd never before had any reason to be prepared.

She'd leave town, naturally, move to Augusta or maybe Columbia. No—farther than that. In fact, the farther away, the better. Of course, she'd have to find work right away and start building up her savings. On the other hand, if she were going to move, it would be foolish to look for a job here. Much better to move first and then—

Out of town papers. She'd go to the library and check the classifieds in all the—

"Joelle! I know damned well you're in there. Let me in!"

Transfixed, Jo stared at the door that was physically rattling under the force of Clay's determined fist. Yanked back from the brink of maternity, she couldn't have answered if her life depended on it.

"I'll fricassee this damned bird of yours if you don't open this door!"

She opened the door. Not that she believed for a minute that he'd have hurt Ivan. The man might have his flaws, but inflicting pain on small feathered creatures wasn't among them. Feeling as if she might shatter at any moment, she reached out her hand for Ivan's traveling cage.

Clay brushed her aside and moved past her. "Would you mind telling me what the hell is going on?" he demanded angrily.

"You're back, so I came home. Thank you for bringing Ivan," she said woodenly.

"I want to know why you ran away."

"I didn't run away, I came home."

"I *know* you came home," he explained, patience eroded long past the breaking point. "What I *don't* know is why! Did I hurt you? Are you afraid of me? Is that it?"

There was no sign of either gentleness or humor. His words were angry, his stance hostile. He hadn't even taken the time to shave, but as Jo stared numbly at the belligerent set of his blue-shadowed jaw, she knew that it wasn't fear that held her in bondage. She'd been instinctively braced against an intolerable hurt. It was either break or bend. She refused to break, but in bending, she began to tremble. The more she trembled, the more fiercely he glared at her.

It was Clay who finally shattered the tableau. Feeling utterly out of his depth, he stared at the maddening creature before him, taking in the unusual pallor of her face, the guarded shadows in her gray-green eyes. She looked as if she'd fracture if he so much as laid a finger on her. Even so, it was all he could do to keep from reaching out and crushing her to him.

Hell, he couldn't trust himself to touch her, even with this splitting headache he'd woken up with. Not after last night. If he touched her, he'd either end up making love to her again or trying to shake some understanding into that stubborn red head of hers. Either way, it would only compound the problem.

It wasn't supposed to happen this way, not at his age. But it had. It had hit him like a ton of bricks. He was crazy in love for the first time in his life, but instead of rushing her to the altar, he was forced to hold back. He had to wait! Normally the most patient of men, Clay had never felt less like waiting in his life.

But if he wanted a lasting relationship—and he couldn't conceive of anything else where Joelle was concerned—then what choice did he have? He was as greedy as the next man when it came to something he wanted badly, but this was different. This was more than mere *wanting*. Any impatience on his part now would be self-defeating in the end. He loved her enough to wait as long as it took. He just hoped it wouldn't take too long.

Exerting all the control he could muster, he said, "Joelle, I think we'd better back off and give this some time, don't you?" He wiped the back of his hand across his forehead and looked vaguely surprised to see it come away quite dry. "Everything's happening too fast."

No, that wasn't it at all. His head kept going around like a damned carousel and his tongue was having trouble coordinating with his brain. "Look, just call me when you're ready to face what we have, will you? Only I'm not as patient as I used to be.'' Raking his hair back from his brow, Clay sent her an agonized look and turned away. He took the steps as if he could hardly wait to get away from her.

"When I'm— Do you actually expect—?'' Jo yelled after him, unable to make sense of her feelings. She closed her eyes and fought down waves of fury.

How could she possibly have thought she was in love with such an insufferable wretch? He was so sure of himself, so certain that when and if she came to her senses, she'd come running after him. Patience? She'd show him patience! Angry words tumbled about in her brain, clumping into the usual bottleneck on their way out. "Don't hold your breath,'' she muttered to the empty stairwell.

March came in with a heat wave that brought everything bursting into bloom at once. For Jo, the days reeled past like a foreign film in black and white, the sound a meaningless jumble. There were no subtitles. There was action; there were shadows and even flashes of light; but there was no color. Breezes laden with flower-petal confetti went unnoticed. Underlying the fragrance of early flowers, the fecund scent of freshly turned earth and the more pungent smell of the river, for once, failed to move her.

She went through the motions, cleaning Ivan's cage twice in a single day, mopping a floor that had already been mopped, ignoring one that had been too long neglected. She read the front page and the classified ads, conscientiously avoiding the editorial page. During the second week it struck her that the *Greensport Daily* had taken on a slightly different appearance. Mostly it was the ads; they were sharper, less cluttered. Evidently the new advertising manager had hit town and was busy making an impression.

"Unlike some others I could name,'' Jo told Ivan. She'd moped long enough. Her family was convinced she had a spring cold. She'd begged off keeping Shannon for a weekend, and when Chip had dropped in with a six-pack, a bag of boiled peanuts and a pound of barbecue to watch a game, she'd chased him off, claiming a splitting headache.

At least she wasn't pregnant. By the time she'd discovered it, she'd made so many contingency plans and conditioned herself to the point where it came as a distinct letdown.

"Some of us weren't born with a full sack of marbles, Ive. Quit rattling your cage, there aren't any more grapes." And unless she hauled herself up out of this slough of despondency, there soon wouldn't be any more birdseed, either. "All right, you noisy old pirate, it's time one of us went back to work. You could dig out your flamingo costume and audition as a yard ornament."

Folding the morning paper to the Help Wanted section, Jo selected a purple marker and began scanning the list. She had worked out a color code, using green for the entries with the most potential, and red for the least. Purple was for everything in between, not that there were that many. It wasn't a long list, and most of the entries were the same old undesirables. At least there was a new listing today.

"Secretarial, too," she told the bird on her shoulder. "Light receptionist duties. If 'light' means opening the door one morning a month, fine. If it's more than that, you might as well forget those grapes I promised you."

It turned out to be more than that. In fact, it was considerably more. But by the time Jo had spent fifty-seven minutes waiting in the reception room of the cramped little Hanover-Boger Clinic, her own problems seemed irrelevant.

"Gee, I'm sorry, Miss...uh, Middleton? We've been going flat out around here ever since—no, Shirley, put her in number four," the assistant administrator interrupted herself to instruct a harried nurse. "I haven't had time to set up in three yet."

"Okay, where were we? I'm Aldean Simmons, by the way. It's this flu thing. C'mon back in the office, there's coffee. Lord, I wish we'd had at least one good freeze last month to kill off all those germs. I don't care what they say, you show me a warm winter, I'll show you a flu epidemic that—"

A damp, bald head poked around the door. "Where the dickens are those forms, Aldean? Didn't you tell them we were out? Call County General and see if you can—" He broke off, bobbed an apologetic greeting to Jo, and said, "If you're the new secretary all I can say is, thank God. Aldean, do we have another chair? It's packed in reception."

Without her knowing quite how it happened, Jo found herself swept into a job that was the last thing she'd ever have chosen. With a whimpering toddler on her lap and an obviously ill mother waiting to be shown to an examining room, she'd had no choice. It could have been Shannon or Chessie whimpering for a mother who was too sick to look after her and unable to hire a baby-sitter.

"Mommie, Mommie, Mommie," the dark-haired tyke droned tearfully.

"Yes, darling, your mommie's right here. She's just going into the next room for a little while. Let's see if we can find something to play with." A box of staples? Hardly. A permanently inked rubber stamp? Mommie wouldn't appreciate that. "Oh, look what I've found," Jo exclaimed, reaching for the tape dispenser. The little girl was soon immersed taping sheets of paper together in a singularly unartistic arrangement.

More people pressed into the reception room, coughing and wheezing and needing attention. Joelle shuffled through the cluttered desk until she found something resembling an appointment book. Most of these people, she'd already discovered, did not have appointments. She'd simply have to play it by ear until she caught on to the system. Or until the epidemic ended. Looking up into the face of an elderly gentleman who was first in line at the window, she smiled and asked his name.

There was little time to be initiated, still less to be intimidated. From the first day on, Jo found herself swept along in the semi-organized madness that seemed to prevail at the small clinic. Most of the patients were on the lower income level, many of them elderly.

In the cluttered office behind a textured glass window, Jo filled out endless forms. To her amazement, she found herself getting involved in the lives of strangers to a degree that would have once been impossible. Both the people she worked with and the people who flocked to the clinic day after day seemed to need her, and because they needed her, she found herself rising to meet that need. Just as she had met the needs of her own family.

There was no room for shyness, not the slightest chance of remaining in the background. She was swept into the microcosm of the clinic from eight until five or six each day, and far too exhausted when the work day ended to worry about whether her personality suited her new job. Or vice versa.

The first week disappeared, and another began. She'd heard nothing from Clay. Other than the perennial ache in the general region of her heart, she'd managed to keep the pain at bay. Any day now she should be strong enough to deal with it; meanwhile, there was a flu epidemic underway, and half the clinic's nurses had been stricken. Everyone was serving double and even triple duty. Including Jo.

During the second week, Jo discovered a new respect for nurses. She was called on to hold howling children for examination and treatment, and support a burly merchant seaman who turned green at the first sight of a needle. She held solemn babies and more wriggling toddlers on her lap while their mothers were being examined, and she filled out in triplicate, quadruplicate and quintuplicate the endless forms. There was a computer crammed into a corner of the cluttered office, but so far no one seemed to have time to get acquainted with it.

Toward the end of the second week, she began to read the editorial pages once more.

The heat wave had given way to a short bout of chilly rainy weather, but then spring bounced back with a series of eighty-degree days. By the time the clinic was once more fully staffed, and Jo was back at filing and billing and helping patients fill out the endless insurance forms, she felt as if she'd worked there for years. She'd not only coped, she'd known a satisfaction that seven years of being a small part of Harriet Brower's Worthy Causes had never come close to producing. With no time to worry about her own silly hang-ups, she'd dealt with problems she hadn't even known existed a month ago. Joelle Middleton had finally come out of the closet.

"Too late, though," as she told Ivan. "Oh, Ive, it hurts. Remember that time I had my wisdom tooth pulled? I was fine for a few days, and then, whammo! I was in agony." The lovebird reached for the top of his open door and hung suspended from a foot while he peered under one wing, waiting for her applause.

Jo, oblivious for once to her pet's need for appreciation, stared morosely at the editorial page. As it happened, she'd saved all the center sections of the paper for the past two weeks—purely by chance, she assured herself. With a bird, one never knew when one might need more newspaper.

Clayton hadn't written a line since—well, just since. She knew; she'd carefully gone back and read every single editorial page. Surely he hadn't left town? His name was still listed in the small box at the top of the page as editor and general manager, along with . . .

"Theresa Leinbach, associate editor," she read aloud.

Jo leaned back, her expression thoughtful. After several minutes, she lowered her gaze to the page once more. Apt quotations from various sources had been a feature of the editorial page for as long as she could remember. Sometimes she skimmed them, usually she skipped them. Something in the one she'd just glanced past caught her eye.

It was by Benjamin Franklin, to the effect that he'd always found satisfaction in going straight forward in doing what appeared to him to be the right thing, and leaving the consequences to Providence.

"The difference between Ben and me, Ive, is that I don't *know* what's right. What does a woman do when she loves a man who ignores her? Was I that big a disappointment? Did he decide I'm not worth the trouble? Was it only the thrill of the chase he was interested in?" In spite of the evidence, she couldn't bring herself to believe that, not about Clay. She knew his mind even better than she knew his body, and she'd have pledged her honor on his integrity.

The trouble was, Jo didn't know enough about men in general. She wished she could trust herself to bring up the subject with Aldean the following day without making a mess of it. They were having lunch together. Aldean, who was divorced, attractive, and had an easygoing warmth that in no way interfered with her almost frightening efficiency, had introduced Jo to a ramshackle place on the river that served the world's best fried fish and hush puppies.

"Neither one of us has to worry about the calories. Besides, the experts have just discovered some magical ingredient in fish that counteracts cholesterol, which makes frying okay again," Aldean said breezily as they examined the cutlery. "This stuff might be stainless, but it's sure not spotless."

"What did you say the sanitation rating was? For a nurse who's supposed to know the dangers, you don't seem very concerned."

"I'm an administrator. I don't have to know anything except how to hang on to my sanity in a mad, mad world."

"As long as you vouch for the food, I won't worry about the silverware. I get so tired of single portions that can be heated in four minutes in a microwave." They laughed together, and then inhaled appreciatively as a waitress passed by with a laden tray.

Jo was wondering how to work the conversation around to the subject of men when she felt it. Electricity—first on her scalp and then on her nape. It was as if someone had tugged every hair on her head at once. She stared intensely at the beads of sweat on her glass of iced tea as the knowledge of Clay's presence settled over her. Just how she knew, she hadn't the faintest idea. She'd never been accused of being psychic. All the same, he was here.

There weren't that many restaurants in Greensport that served good food, Jo reminded herself, trying to tame the erratic response of her heartbeat. It was inevitable that she'd run into him sooner or later once she was no longer munching a sandwich over her typewriter in Harriet's converted sunroom. Only now that she had, she wasn't ready.

"Hello, Jo."

Resigned, she turned her head and looked up in the direction of that deep, familiar voice. "Hello, Clay." Her eyes widened, and before she could stop herself, she blurted out, "You look awful!"

He was gray and drawn, and he looked as if he'd lost several pounds. But his eyes had lost none of their brilliance, and his smile, while a bit tentative, still had the power to paralyze her brain.

Had she thought she'd developed a certain immunity? Oh, Lord, how we mortals delude ourselves. Breathe in, breathe out, Jo ordered herself frantically. Smile and see if your face cracks. There, that wasn't so bad, was it? Somewhat to her amazement, she found that she was able to draw from newly developed resources. She reached out to indicate the extra chair at their table. "Sit down before you drop, Clay. This is Aldean Simmons, my administrator. I mean, where I work. The administrator there, I mean. Oh, darn."

"Nice to meet you, Ms. Simmons," Clay said, turning his smile toward the older woman. He continued to stand, and frantically, Jo began to wonder if she'd been too forward.

"You're working again, then?" he asked, turning back to Jo. Was it her imagination, or were his eyes really burning holes in her skin? It was probably her face that was burning—as usual.

"At the clinic on River Street. Hanover-Boger. For two weeks."

"Do you like it?" Are you happy? he wanted to ask her? Have you thought about me? Have you lain awake at night the way I have, wondering if it was all a part of the delirium?

How could he stand there swapping meaningless phrases, with half the town looking on, when he wanted to snatch her up in his arms and carry her off to somewhere quiet and private, where they could be alone together for the next millenium? Dammit, after two weeks of flu he was so weak he could barely support his own weight. He lacked the strength to pull off any grand, or even semigrand, gestures.

He wouldn't be here now except that he'd been putting Theresa off ever since she'd arrived. This was in the nature of a trial run. Today was the first day he'd been able to work more than a few hours, and he'd planned to call Jo if he held up all right and ask her out tomorrow night.

While he considered the best way to handle the situation, the waitress brought two baskets of smoking hot french fries and fish, and another of golden hush puppies and placed them on the table.

"Please do join us, Mr. Abbott," Aldean invited, her warm hazel eyes openly interested.

"I'm sorry, I—"

"Clay? Are we joining your friends?" Jo recognized the voice immediately. It was the same one she'd taken a message from over the phone, a message she'd never bothered to pass on. Was there a back door to this place? Could she manage to slide under the table, crawl around the end booth and reach the kitchen without causing too much of a stir?

Clay made the introductions, and Jo found her hand being clasped in the firm grip of an attractive, auburn-haired woman dressed in a peach-colored linen jacket over a full-skirted dress in a misty pastel floral. Her heart sank. Newspaper women were supposed to dress in cast iron coat suits, not tea-party costumes. No wonder Clay had dropped from sight. No wonder he hadn't written anything in weeks. From the looks of him, he'd been burning the candle at both ends.

That damned candle! Him and his limericks. Jo told herself she sincerely wished she'd never met the man, but in the next instant, she knew that was a lie. "Aldean, I just remembered that I'm expecting a COD shipment of file folders and copy paper today. Could we take these baskets back to the clinic with us? Maybe they have some take-out plates—or you could stay and—"

Her shoulders slumped in defeat. Who could blame the man for preferring five-feet-five with plenty of curves over five-feet-nine and built like a flagpole? What man would want to run his fingers through a copper scouring pad when he could sift through soft, auburn waves? The woman didn't even have a freckle, not a single blemish!

God, she would have to go and fall in love with a man with good taste. Why couldn't she have picked another lemon who'd have been satisfied with something less than perfection? *Far* less, she added with ruthless self-honesty.

"Look, don't let us disturb you," Clay said easily. "We already have a table, and we're expecting someone to join us. Ms. Simmons, nice meeting you. Jo...?" His smile was tentative, involving his eyes more than his lips.

She hadn't imagined it, Jo told herself after Clay and his guest had moved on. He had been studying her as if she were a particularly fascinating blob on a slide under a microscope. Even Aldean had noticed it.

"What's between you two?" she whispered, leaning across the table.

"Your bosom is getting buttered," Jo observed dryly. "There's nothing between us, why did you think there was?"

"Oh, come *on*, honey. If you don't want to talk about it, that's your privilege, but don't tell me nothing's going on. I can smell smoke from a mile away."

"Yes, well...Clay happens to have a very effective sprinkler system, so any sparks have been thoroughly doused."

"Did Miss Peaches and Cream have anything to do with it?"

"Theresa Leinbach?" Jo shrugged, prodded a crusty chunk of fish and pushed her basket away. "Not really. Maybe. How do I know?"

Aldean waited. When it became evident that Jo wasn't going to elaborate, she reached for the check. "Want a doggy bag? You didn't do Katy's Kitchen justice."

All Jo wanted was to get back to the clinic where she could throw herself into coming to terms with the electronic monster who was supposed to make life easier for them all. The thing was forever on the blink, and the last secretary hadn't trusted it any more than Jo did. She'd kept a complete set of books and records, which was fortunate, for Jo had forgotten what little she'd learned in business school about computers.

Her concentration was shot. She made appointments, answered questions, and filled out forms, but afterward she couldn't remember a single thing about the rest of that afternoon. All except for the pain. It had dwindled to a dull ache that was almost bearable until she'd seen him again. Now she was afraid she'd never feel well again.

After a lapse of two weeks, one of Clay's editorials appeared on the day after she'd seen him in Katy's Kitchen. Even to Jo's prejudiced eye it lacked his usual punch. Too many distractions, she told herself, feeling even more miserable than before, if that was possible.

Against all reason, she had hoped he'd come by after work, or at least call her. Her mind told her hope was a luxury she could no longer afford, but that didn't stop her from running to the door when she heard footsteps on the stairs, or breaking her neck to answer the phone on the second ring. The footsteps were those of her upstairs neighbor, the phone call from Fran, who wanted to know if she was over her cold, or if it had turned into the flu.

She was completely unprepared for the familiar envelope, addressed in the bold, black scrawl, that fell out of her bundle of junk mail the next day. Not even waiting to let

Ivan out of his cage and put away the groceries she'd bought with her first pay check, she ripped it open, having recognized the handwriting immediately.

The first thing she saw was the RSVP at the lower corner. Lifting her gaze, she read the five lines.

> A newspaper man from GA
> Met a lady who couldn't say nay.
> In allowing her space,
> He fell flat on his face,
> Now he doesn't know quite what to say.

Jo reread the words several times, trying on various interpretations. *A lady who couldn't say "nay"?* Well, that one was easy enough—she hated the term, but she couldn't deny that she'd been a pushover all her life. That had been part of the problem between them. She'd changed, but of course, Clay couldn't know that.

He fell flat on his face? Did that mean he regretted having made love to her? From pacing, Jo dropped onto the sofa. When Ivan rattled his bell and issued a shrill demand, she got up again and opened the cage door.

"Well, what else could it mean? You tell me, you're the expert in these matters. More to the point, what does he expect me to do about it now?" she demanded of the lovebird who appeared to be reading over her shoulder. "RSVP? What does that mean, Request you Save your Virginity, Please? It's hardly a condition that can be declared retroactive."

Ivan flew to the coffee table and perched on the rim of a porcelain pitcher, systematically removing the petals from the jonquils and narcissus a grateful patient had given Jo for straightening out a long-standing hassle with his insurance company.

"Stop eating my flowers you turkey, you know what they do to your system." Jo fished around under the sofa and came up with a peanut to use as a distraction. "It's a little late for regrets," she went on, her voice thickening as her eyes began to sting. If he hadn't meant it, he shouldn't have done it.

Limericks. He thought he could bow out gratefully with a clever limerick, did he? She'd give him limericks! "A social disaster named Jo," she ventured experimentally, "Was dealt a most serious blow." Shaking her head, she began again. "A redheaded wimp from Greensport, who was hardly an aggressive sort . . ."

And then she crumpled. Dammit, she was as bad as he was. Neither one of them could finish what they started.

Ivan hopped from the coffee table to her knee and waddled up her arm, settling himself in the curve of her neck. Ignoring his attempts to comfort her by grooming her hair, she keeled over on the sofa and gave in to the tears that had been held in abeyance for too long.

Ten

Jo's bout of tears was fierce, if brief. Afterward, she stood under a warm shower, gradually letting it run cold. Shivering, she quickly dried herself and dressed in a faded sleeveless sweatshirt and a pair of jogging pants Chip had discarded when he'd had to give up working for the recreation department. Held up by a drawstring, they billowed about her slender hips like a gray balloon. A pair of white cotton socks completed her lounging attire.

Working with every appearance of cheerfulness, she crisped fresh string beans in the microwave for Ivan and herself. They shared conveniently similar tastes in green vegetables. Still moving briskly, she dumped a small block of frozen lasagna into a tiny casserole and set the time for four minutes.

The phone rang. "Get that, will you, Ivan? If it's for me,

tell them to leave a message." She scooped up the lasagna carton on her way to answer it.

"I need to talk to you," Clay said without preamble.

Jo's lungs compressed. She gripped the phone in one hand and the empty carton in the other. "Hello, Clay," she said, amazed to discover that her vocal cords were still functioning even if her wits had suddenly deserted her.

"Look, are you doing anything tonight?"

"No, not—I mean, nothing," she stammered. Brain damage. The would account for it.

"Then may I—? Or if you'd rather, we could..." He took a deep breath and tried again. "What I'm trying to say is, we could talk over dinner if you'd like."

Like a tipsy tightrope walker, Jo's emotions teetered wildly between laughter and tears. "I just put a frozen lasagna in the microwave." *Forget your silly lasagna, you idiot, just say yes!*

"How big is it?"

"How big? I'm not sure, does one cubic foot sound about right?" She clutched the phone in a damp hand and tried to think of something witty and urbane to say before he hung up in disgust.

"Your lasagna, not your oven! Forget it, I'll bring something. I mean, may I come over? Look, just wait right there, will you?" She distinctly heard the rasp of an exaggerated sigh. "Oh, hell, it must be catching. I'm beginning to sound like you."

Jo's laughter was a bit uneven. "I think I've just been insulted."

"If you can think at all, that's more then I've been able to manage lately. Twenty minutes, all right?"

"Clay, I'm not even— Make it an hour!" Her gaze darted frantically around the room. She usually tackled her housework when she got home from the clinic. She'd been so apathetic since seeing Clay that she hadn't bothered.

"Thirty minutes," he countered.

"Forty-five." She was a wreck. Her hair was still wet, she was wearing an elephant suit, and she had a broken nail. Actually, she was rather proud of the latter. It was the first time she could ever remember having a fingernail long enough to break.

The minute he hung up, Jo flew into action, tossing the crumpled carton she still held onto a nearby bookshelf and snatching a handful of dead leaves off Maureen. That done, she dashed into the bedroom and began dragging clothes from the closet, tossing one outfit after another aside, unable to find anything even faintly presentable. Where was her fairy godmother when she really needed her?

"Oh, Lord...shoes!" She had three pairs of sneakers, two pairs of serviceable, comfortable flats, and two pairs of dressy shoes, one too wintry and one too summery.

The ping of a timer bell announced that her supper was done, and a fresh problem struck her. There were plenty of string beans, and she'd made her usual herbed yogurt dip, but a single-serving entree wouldn't go very far. Unless she cooked another one just like it and mixed them together. With a little more cheese on top, he'd probably never know the difference.

Unmindful of the green suede shoes she still clutched in one hand, she hurried to the kitchen and rummaged through the freezer compartment. "Turnip greens, chicken and...chicken? No lasagna. Okay, how about a casserole of lasagna and Chicken Orientale? Maybe a side dish of instant grits?"

Ivan replied with a shrill arpeggio, ending abruptly when the doorbell buzzed. Jo groaned. "Already? He promised me forty-five minutes." Distraught, she glanced at her watch. "Damn!" she muttered softly. She'd a good mind to let him cool his heels for the next thirty-three minutes. But then he'd leave, and she'd either go running after him or sit there and wither away, like her poor unwatered Maureen. Neither alternative held much appeal. The trouble was, she no sooner managed to erect a few barriers, than he showed up and knocked them all down again.

Tucking the shoes under her arm, but still holding the frozen dinner, she hurried to let him in. "Sybil?" Jo's puzzled gaze dropped to the cherub who was attacking her kneecap with a chocolate chip cookie, and she knelt to gather her niece up in her arms. "What are you all doing here?"

"As greetings go, I've heard better, even from you. Here, if you've got Shannon, let me take that stuff." Sybil Turner tossed a large plastic shopping bag onto the coffee table and reached for Jo's shoes and the package of frozen chicken. "We've been shopping," she said. "Shannon's outgrown everything she owns, and Chessie's hand-me-downs never do fit right."

"Chessie takes after me."

"And little Miss Butterfat takes after her mommie and her aunt Fran. As usual, everything that fits around the middle is miles too long, so I hope you're feeling up to doing a few hems. It's just four pair of overalls and a couple of dresses. Three inches on the pants, about two on the dresses. The way she's growing, you'll be letting them out again in a few weeks."

Jo had always done hems for all the children, as she was the only one in the family who could even thread a needle. The only one foolish enough to admit to it, at any rate.

Sybil lifted her carefully groomed brows at the shoes in her hand, dropped them near the sofa, and carried the frozen entree to the kitchen, leaving it in the sink. "You look tired, honey. New job getting you down?"

"No, it's great. It's just that—"

"Just that what?"

Jo hesitated, knowing that the mere mention of a man's name would bring on one of Sybil's inquisitions. "I thought you were someone else, that's all. Come on, baby, let's get rid of that cookie before Nant Jo has chocolate chip hair. Want to help me slice an apple for Ivan?"

"Who were you expecting, if I'm not being too nosy?" Sybil collected a wad of waxed paper from the bookshelf and deposited it in the kitchen trash. "Honestly, Jo, sometimes I wonder about you. Living alone, you get into such slovenly habits."

"Thanks," Jo said dryly. Retrieving the Chicken Orientale from the sink, she popped it back into the freezer, sliced an apple, and handed one of the wedges to Shannon. "Watch fingers, honey. We'll just put a slice in the cage and let Ivan help himself, all right?"

"By the way," Sybil remarked, leafing through the stack of junk mail on the cluttered coffee table, "I never did find out what happened to that good-looking newspaper man who helped you baby-sit the night Oscar and I went out with the Handleys. Fran really had her hopes up, but I told her..."

Good looking? Fran's new Chesterfield coat was good-looking. The new pink tapestry on Sybil's Queen Anne wing chair was good-looking. Clayton Abbott was stunning, magnificent, superlative!

Jo waited. "You told her what?" She could well imagine the directions Sybil's comments had taken. With a total lack of malice, her older sister never failed to deflate whatever small triumphs Jo managed to achieve.

"Oh, just that—" Sybil lifted her shoulders in an expressive gesture. "Well, let's face it, hon, he was a little too rich for your blood, wasn't he?"

"For your information—" Jo broke off to snatch Shannon's chubby fingers from the danger zone before Ivan could add a bit of protein to his diet. "Oh, forget it. Come on, sweety, let's go swab you down before the ants discover you." She took a sticky hand and led her niece to the bathroom, forcing herself to see the humorous side of the situation. There had to be one somewhere. She just had to look a little harder to find it.

Jo was still in the bathroom with Shannon when Oscar arrived. From the living room, she heard the pleasant male voice she'd once thought the most beautiful in all creation. God, what an endless adolescence she'd endured. She'd finally begun to have hopes of working her way through it before senility set in, but maybe she'd been too optimistic.

Jo squirted hand lotion onto one tiny, starfish-shaped palm and sat the bottle back on the shelf. Adolescence to senescence, she mused. There was material for a limerick there somewhere. She might even tackle it sometime when she wasn't quite so depressed—or frustrated.

"Rub the rest on your cheeks—no, not your hair, sweety. Let's go show your daddy what a clean, sweet-smelling little girl you are." How on earth could she get rid of three people in the next two minutes without resorting to rudeness? On second thought, what was wrong with a little rudeness? This was an emergency.

"Hello, Oscar, what brings you here?" Jo settled for borderline rude. If that didn't work, she'd try something a little less subtle—like a fire hose.

"Oh, hi, Joelle, did you finally get over your cold, or whatever?" Without pausing to hear her response, he turned back to his wife. "I figured you'd shop till they pushed you out the mall door, and then come by here to drop off whatever needed alterations. You and Shannon take my car on home, honey, and I'll go by the garage with yours and get the front end aligned. I don't like the way those tires have been wearing."

Jo, with Shannon slung across one hip, studied her brother-in-law with fond exasperation. He really hadn't changed much in all the years she'd known him. Not nearly as much as she had. It occurred to her that, like a dormant plant, she'd been gathering strength for years, waiting only for the right stimulus before bursting into bloom, ready to bear fruit.

"Bear fruit?" she murmured in amazement. Lord, where had that idea sprung from? Before she could come up with an answer, she was distracted by the sound of another set of footsteps coming up the stairs.

Clay! The place was a wreck—she was a wreck, and Shannon had just untied her drawstring. What had she done to deserve all this?

"Bear what fruit?" asked Sybil with a puzzled frown.

"What? Oh—*buy* fruit," she invented wildly. "Apples! I need to get more apples tomorrow." It was starting already, and she hadn't even had time to enjoy her postadolescent years. She looked desperately at her brother-in-law. "What time does the garage close? Hadn't you better hurry?" The footsteps paused outside her door. Jo fumbled to retie her drawstring, hoisted Shannon to her shoulder, and with a last fleeting thought for the turquoise dress she'd wanted Clay to see her in, opened it.

Chip breezed in with a wide grin for Jo, a teasing remark for Sybil, and a wisecrack for Oscar. After the first moment of confusion, Jo ignored him. Her gaze had already lighted on the man who had followed him up the stairs. "It hasn't been forty-five minutes," she protested.

A murmur of voices behind her rose and fell unheeded as she tumbled headlong into the blue depths of Clay's eyes. "I wasn't expecting them," she said hurriedly, wincing as Shannon gave up tugging on the label at the back of her shirt and turned her attentions to a vulnerable section of hair at Jo's temple. "Honey, that hurts. Don't play rough, all right?"

"P'ay wuff, p'ay wuff," the child chanted.

"Come play rough with uncle Chip, okay, muffin? Looks like Aunt Jo's got other fish to fry right now."

Jo relinquished the child with a warning scowl. "Thanks, Chip. What did you want, anyway? Is there a game tonight?"

"Just dropped by to see if you were better," Chip said breezily, swinging Shannon up to the ceiling.

"Than what?" Who invited all these people to her tea party, dammit?

"Than you were the last time you bit my head off. Are you over whatever ailed you?" His knowing grin swung toward the door where Clay hovered, looking ready to bolt at any moment.

Feeling as if she'd tumbled headlong into a Lewis Carrol novel, Jo managed to get through the introductions. "Please—don't let me rush you off, Chip," she said hopefully.

Over Shannon's squeals, Sybil was going on about hems and thread colors and doing the yellow first when Oscar edged through the noisy huddle near the door. "Abbott, good to see you again. Oscar Turner. You came with Jo to our house to baby-sit one night last month, remember? Thought to myself at the time, that's one thing not many young ladies can brag about, being baby-sat by the managing editor of the best daily paper in east Georgia. Jo, your phone's ringing, want me to get it?''

"I don't believe this.'' Jo whispered. With a despairing look at Clay, she dashed across the room, nearly tripping in her haste. Snatching up the phone, she turned back toward the door, praying that Clay wouldn't give up in disgust and walk out. When he'd asked if she was doing anything tonight, she hadn't counted on the whole Middleton clan descending on her. All she needed now was for Fran and her crew and Hal to drop in.

Clay followed her progress across the room, saw her almost trip over a shoe and fling him a harried look over her shoulder. It was the look that made him decide to stick it out, mob scene or no mob scene. If she could put up with her family *en masse*, then he could, too. He was beginning to see why she'd never stood a chance with this bunch, though. They all talked at once, and nobody listened.

"Mike? Sorry, I can't hear you, you'll have to speak up.''

From near the front door, Clay strained to hear what was being said without being too obvious about it.

"Somebody I know is getting fussy. You'd better get her fed before she gets too sleepy,'' Oscar was saying nearby. "Come on, I'll switch the car seat for you. What about that bag on the coffee table, is that yours?''

"It stays. Jo's going to hem everything. Oh, I forgot to tell her about shortening the straps on the pink gingham sun suit, but I guess that can wait. Clay,'' Sybil whispered loudly as she squeezed past him in the doorway, "Tell Jo to remember to hem the yellow first, all right? Shannon's play group is having their picture made next Tuesday, and Shannon looks adorable in yellow.''

Clay nodded, his ears still tuned to what was being said on the other side of the room. "But Mike, I—" he heard her say.

"Hey, look, if you and Jo have plans for tonight," Chip said, "maybe I'd better be shoving off, too. I just thought I'd stop by and see if she could keep Chipper a couple of nights next month. There's a convention at Paradise Island in the Bahamas, and Candy and I thought we might sort of make an occasion of it, you know what I mean? Tell Jo not to make plans for the weekend of the eighth, okay?''

Chip left just as Jo was saying, "I'm sorry, Mike. Maybe one of the nurses can shop for you, I don't have time.'' She hung up the phone and turned around, her troubled gaze colliding with Clay's watchful one.

It occurred to him that eyes that clear should be against the law. Closing the door on the receding chatter, he moved toward her, stopping just short of the point of no return. Every instinct told him that if he so much as laid a hand on her, he wouldn't have a snowball's chance of keeping his head.

"I'm sorry about the invasion." Suddenly feeling acutely self-conscious now that they were alone, Jo let her gaze wander from the shoe on the floor to its mate on the coffee table, and then to the shopping bag Sybil had left behind. There was half a chocolate chip cookie on a chair arm, and she swept it into her palm and then stared at it helplessly until Clay took it from her and dropped it into a flowerpot.

"Clean house later if it bothers you.''

"It's a mess—I'm a mess. I'd meant to put on something—" She gestured vaguely to the shapeless gray sweatsuit that enveloped her. "But then everybody just sort of...materialized, and it was too late." Her eyes begged his forbearance, hardly daring to hope for more. His own chambray shirt and chinos could hardly be described as dressy, yet he couldn't have looked more impressive in white tie and tails.

"Does it happen often?"

"The mess? Oh...the invasion. Often enough." The words they were speaking seemed to bear no relation to the messages their eyes were sending. Jo felt the hollowness in her chest expand until breathing became a conscious effort.

"By the way, you're to do the yellow first," Clay said, his deep voice a little more raw than she remembered it. "The play group's having their picture taken on Tuesday. Oh, and keep the weekend of the eighth clear."

"The yellow first." Jo nodded, her gaze never leaving his face. "What happens on the weekend of the eighth?" The hollowness had seeped down to invade her legs, which made standing a considerable risk. She dropped down on one end of the sofa.

"You're to keep something called a chipper. Another bird?"

"A nephew," Jo said with a sigh. "And I won't. Candy's mom loves to have an excuse to come stay, but Chipper always gripes because she makes him do his homework before he watches TV."

"And you don't?" Clay sat just far enough away to be safe, close enough so that he could catch an occasional drift of the clean, feminine scent of her skin. Every day he hadn't seen her seemed like a year. Her hair was still the same wild, glorious tangle that made his fingers itch to tame it, her face, faintly freckled, innocent of artifice, was as delicately molded as ever. Yet he sensed something different about her.

"Discipline was never my strong suit," Jo said huskily.

"No, I imagine not. What did the ex-fiancé want?"

"He needs a nightshirt. He claims he can't wear pajamas over the contraption on his knee, and hospital gowns are too drafty."

"You declined," said Clay with a smile.

"You listened."

"That's two out of three; the nays have it. Congratulations."

"That's right—nay to Mike and Chipper, yea to Shannon's hems." Jo's face was solemn, but her gray-green eyes began to glow with satisfaction. "Of course, there was a lot of room for improvement," she said modestly. "They all need to learn not to be so dependent. Maybe if I wean them gradually, it won't be long before they can stand alone."

Was she putting him on? There wasn't a hint of a smile on those soft, pink lips of hers, and yet . . .

It was her eyes that gave her away, those fathomless crystal pools that reflected her thoughts and feelings with such devastating clarity. They were dancing with laughter.

The little devil! It was those unexpected flashes of humor that had fascinated him from the very first. Somewhere deep inside him, Clay felt an invisible bond of constraint begin to dissolve.

Jo drew her knees up beside her on the sofa in an unconscious effort to erect a small barrier between them. Something in the way he was looking at her made her shift uneasily. "Are you hungry? I am," she said brightly.

"Ravenous." The grin that creased his lean cheeks—leaner now than she remembered them—turned the words into a parody of a leer.

"Ivan and I could share our string bean salad with you," she offered. "And if you like frozen lasagna or Chicken Orientale, you're in luck."

On hearing his name, the lovebird began to vocalize at the top of his piercing voice. Clay winced. "Rudy might be loud, but at least he doesn't shatter your eardrums."

"Oh, Ivan'll not only shatter your drums, he'll even pierce your ears. There's no end to his talents." After placating the lovebird with a string bean and a few pumpkin seeds, Jo excused herself to change clothes.

Rising, Clay caught her hand. "Not on my account. You're fine just the way you are," he assured her. His hands moved to her shoulders, slipping under the fleecy material of her sleeveless shirt. A tingling awareness entered the atmosphere. "Make yourself too irresistible," he murmured, "and you might not get fed."

As the heat of his hands seared Jo's shoulders, a series of tremors threatened to undermine her will. She needed to change into something, all right, armor, layers and layers of it! "Clay," she pleaded weakly. "I was beginning to get myself sorted out, but if you're going to do *that*..."

"This?" Leaning forward, he placed his forehead against hers as his hands tightened on her shoulders.

Oh, please, I'm not ready for this. I need more time! Don't kiss me, please don't, Jo pleaded silently. "Please kiss me," her traitorous voice said, and in defeat, she leaned against him.

Clay laughed softly, and Jo watched his eyes go from noonday-to midnight-blue in one flaring moment. "I thought you'd never ask," he murmured just before his lips came down on hers.

His mouth was hungry, his arms hardening until the muscles bit into her ribs. Jo clung to him as ecstasy blinded her to all but the reality that was Clay. She couldn't get close enough—all that billowing fabric between them!

"I've missed you so," he uttered hoarsely against her lips. His hand slipped down her back, curved over her bottom, and with a deep sigh, he spread his feet apart and fitted her against his thighs. "I wanted to explain—"

"I don't need explanations, I only need you to hold me."

"Only hold you?" Clay taunted gently. "Sweetheart, even at my prime, that might be too tall an order."

Jo worked a hand between them and began tugging at the buttons on his shirt. With her head buried under his chin, she stroked the tanned vee of his throat with the tip of her tongue, and felt his whole body stiffen. "I'm not sure what you call 'prime'..."

"Full strength...stamina—forget it! I'll explain later. Ah, yes, that's right, don't stop," he said with a small groan when she finally managed to work one hand through the opening of his shirt.

After savoring the textures, the heat and the strength of him in an exploratory pass over his chest, she let her hand play downward. Boldly, driven by the wanton stranger who had taken control of her mind and body, Jo nudged the constriction of his belt with her fingertips, loving the way the rigid slab of his abdomen jerked in response to her probing.

"Here, let me—" Clay broke off, and with a swift movement, divested them both of their shirts. Holding her at arms length, he struggled to get his breath as his gaze played over her pale slenderness, lingering on the high, taut breasts that were already pouting with arousal. She hadn't been wearing a bra under the fleecy cotton, and the tips of her nipples were deep rose against the palest pink. "Oh, God, you're even more wonderful than I remembered," he whispered. "All those feverish dreams when I didn't know if I was awake or asleep, I kept picturing you like this."

Held in the quivering suspension of desire, Jo could actually feel his gaze on her, feel the sweet, slow pressures hammering low in her body. Feverish dreams? Had he had those, too?

"But aren't your trousers supposed to be a little more transparent, my darling houri?"

Glancing down at her baggy drawstring pants, Jo bit her lip. "If you don't care for them..." she suggested, and he took the hint. With one swift tug, the drawstring came undone, and he used the ends to pull her tightly against him once more. With Jo's arms clinging around his neck, Clay slipped his hands over her bottom to press her hips against him. Slowly, with infinite care, he eased the trousers down until they puddled about her feet. Along the way, he caressed and explored and aroused until Jo could barely stand.

"Your turn," he informed her, his voice a constricted whisper. Unwinding her arms from around his neck, he placed her hands on his belt. "I'm a firm believer in a fair division of—"

"Labor?" Jo finished for him, her fingers already fumbling at the unfamiliar workings of his buckle. She'd never been very mechanical and now she could have screamed in frustration.

"Pleasure," he corrected. "Would it help if I turned around?" Holding one of her arms, he turned so that she was pressed against his back. Then he drew both her arms around his waist. "Pretend it's your own belt and zipper."

With his firm buttocks pressing into her soft abdomen, his hard, warm back under her cheek, he was asking the impossible. Jo's thumb inadvertently raked his navel. He groaned; she gasped. His dry, hard hands covered hers, and under his guidance, she finally managed to unsnap the brass-and-ebony buckle.

The tab of a zipper nudged her fingertips. Gingerly, she began to ease it downward, her heart fluttering somewhere in the vicinity of her throat at the slow, rasping sound. Then she froze. Neither of them moved. As if unable to help himself, Clay covered her hand with his, flattening her palm over the hard ridge for an instant before removing his own hand.

He was giving her a chance to escape. Jo could feel the powerful thunder of his heart, the raw sound of his indrawn breath. Driven by a compulsion stronger than anything she'd ever known, she let her hand linger, explore—caress.

She heard his breath whistle through his teeth, and then he moaned. "Ah, Joelle, that feels so good!" Wildly aroused, she reached her other hand upward, tracing the rigid contours of his stomach, combing through the wiry hair to find what she sought. She rolled his tiny nipple between her thumb and forefinger, glorying in the intensely masculine response that shuddered throughout his body. Pressing her parted lips to his back, she tasted his flesh, raked it with her teeth, and reveled in her power to bring such pleasure to another mortal.

A series of hard tremors shook him as he struggled for control, and then he carefully lifted her hands away from his body and turned her in his arms. His mouth came down on hers with a fierce and desperate hunger that could no longer go unassuaged. While she was still reeling from his kiss, Clay bent her over his arm to follow the arch of her throat with his mouth, tasting, nipping, until he reached her breast.

"Oh, please," Jo gasped, shuddering as a spasm of pleasure shot through her. He stabbed her hardened nipple repeatedly with the moist spear of his tongue, and then drew it into his mouth. "Clay, I can't—take much more."

"Oh, sweetheart, do you think I can?" Sweeping her up into his arms, he considered the two closed doors, unerringly choosing the one that led to her bedroom. Looking darkly alien against her familiar white wicker, the green and white sprigged wallpaper and the pale peach accessories, he lowered her to the waiting bed. Jo lifted her arms invitingly.

"Let me just get something from my pants pocket. I won't be a minute," he promised.

Not pretending to misunderstand, Jo shook her head. "You don't have to, Clay. Working at the clinic, I— Oh, please, just hurry and love me. I think I'm starting to melt."

With one searching look, Clay knelt, kissing her shoulders, her breasts, the exquisitely vulnerable place at the side of her throat. Then, lifting his head, he closed his eyes briefly, trying valiantly to hang on to a shred of control. "I wanted to go slower," he whispered harshly. "But I need you so much it's killing me!"

Jo could see the tendons standing out at the side of his throat, the flush that darkened the angular planes of his cheeks. "Clay," she said, unable to stem the words that overflowed her heart. "I love you so. Please..."

It was over much too quickly. He thought he'd said the words, but maybe he'd only thought them. God knows, they were burned so deeply into his own consciousness that they were a part of his very soul.

She'd lifted her hips, and he'd sheathed himself swiftly in her satiny depths. They were both so close to the edge by then that he'd felt it beginning almost at once. He'd tried to hold back, tried to make it last, but when her fingernails bit into his shoulders and she looked at him that way—startled, almost disbelieving, he was lost. By the time she closed her eyes, her pupils had almost eclipsed the silver of her irises.

A whimper escaped her, and he captured it with his lips, driven to possess the very essence of her, the sound, the scent, the feel of her long, slender legs wrapped around his waist. Thrusting, withdrawing, and thrusting to the limit, he gathered her in his arms and rolled over onto his side, allowing her to set the pace. Almost immediately, the shuddering spasms deep inside her pushed him beyond the limits of endurance, and the last shred of his control snapped.

Clinging tightly, they rode the crest, allowing it to wash over them as they drowned in a sea of indescribable pleasure. Not until the last small ripple had subsided did Clay speak.

"Did you really mean that?" he murmured deeply.

Jo nuzzled his throat drowsily. "Did I mean what?"

"What you said, that you love me?"

There it was again, that old familiar urge to slip away and hide herself. Having abandoned herself so completely only moments before, she now felt incredibly vulnerable. As if she'd suddenly found herself in a public place, stark naked. He'd said he needed her; she'd told him she loved him.

Semantics, the new Jo told herself forcefully. Ignoring the shadow of insecurity that would probably be with her all her life, she snuggled into the shelter of the arms that held her. "I love you, Clay. There, I can even say it without stammering. Can you?" she whispered after the merest hesitation.

Clay laughed softly, his hands lazily exploring the contours of her back. "Of course I can, darling." He held her away from him so that he could kiss the tip of her elegant little nose. Freckled elegance—she delighted him in every conceivable way. "How do you want it? In limerick form? Sky writing? Shall I take out a full-page ad, or maybe a billboard?"

"A simple declarative sentence will do just fine."

"I could teach Rudy to say it for me," he suggested hopefully.

"What's the matter, are you shy?" Jo wriggled closer.

Clay grinned. Yeah, come to think of it, maybe he was. It was one thing to sit in his office and spill his innermost thoughts onto paper, another thing altogether to speak them aloud. "Ironic, isn't it? Must be a side effect from the flu."

Jo's head bobbed up from the pillow of his shoulder. "The flu! *You?* But when? Why didn't you—? Clay, are you all right?"

"Yes, the flu, me, and last week," he answered indulgently. "Or was it the week before? I lost track of time."

"Are you all right now? You shouldn't be exerting yourself so soon afterward."

"A little late to be worried about exertion, isn't it?" he teased. "I woke up with it the morning after—after I got back from Atlanta, only I didn't know what it was for a day or so. Thought I was just exhausted. You mean you didn't catch it?"

The flu. Then that accounted for his being so groggy that night, and for his staying away for so long. He'd told her they needed to take some time to think, but she hadn't really expected him to— "What? Oh. I told you I was healthy as a horse," she dismissed. "I have lots of resistance to practically everything."

"Oh, do you now?" Clay trailed his fingers across her shoulder and over her breast in a seemingly random pattern.

Jo gasped as he searched out each sensitive place on her body and proceeded to tune her nerves to bowstring tautness. "Well," she conceded breathlessly, "resistance to *some* things. Clay, why didn't you let me know? I would have come."

"I know you would have, darling. That's one of the reasons I didn't ask. You never could say no. The other was that I was too damned sick, and I didn't want you to see me that way.

"Who took care of you?"

"I did."

Jo ached at the thought. "Who took care of the birds?"

"Who do you think? Paid for it with a relapse, which meant that my new staff on the paper had to wing it. I've tried to make it up to them over the past few days, at least help get them sorted out and settled in. You met Theresa at Katy's Kitchen, remember? She's good. She'll be great if she ever gets her love life sorted out." He grinned. "Once I got over the worst of it, I did some scribbling. I wanted to write you a sonnet. It seemed the least I could do in declaring myself was to use proper form."

Jo sat up in bed beside him, completely oblivious to her nudity, and gazed down at him expectantly. *How do I love thee, let me count the ways?*

"Unfortunately, it came out another limerick—not a very romantic one, at that." Clay's rueful expression begged forgiveness, and she laughed away the small surge of disappointment.

She'd liked to have heard the words—just three simple words, in sonnet form or any form. He could put it in a recipe for all she cared, if only he'd tell her. She leaned over and propped her elbows on his chest. "Was that the one you sent me?"

"Oh, that. One of my lesser works," he dismissed. "I think the second attempt went something like this."

> "A man who was longing to woo
> Was struck down in mid-woo by the flu
> His thoughts were X-rated,
> His body prostrated,
> His timing completely askew."

She had to laugh. "If I can't have a sonnet, I'll take a limerick about your X-rated thoughts any day."

"One of these days I'll manage to write you a sonnet. Probably reams of them, all bad."

"It's the thought that counts," Jo comforted. "However if you want to work on a sonnet, you could try out a few simple words. Just a single line to start with."

"Like what?"

"Like you know what," she said pointedly.

"Now? You mean the actual words? Out of context?"

"The actual words, and what does context have to do with anything?" She was beginning to enjoy watching him squirm. Clayton Abbott, *shy?* Never in a million years. And yet, he had every earmark.

"Out loud?"

"Out loud."

"I do much better with limericks," he said hopefully.

"You mean you hide behind them," Jo retorted.

"You said you liked my limericks."

"I *love* your limericks," she corrected. She stretched out beside him, arms crossed under her head, thoroughly enjoying his discomfiture. Who would have suspected a man like Clay could be so vulnerable? "All right, try another limerick. See if you can bring yourself to use the actual

words this time. Shyness isn't terminal, you know. I recovered. You probably will, too, but you have to work on
it.'' She was trying hard to ignore the weight of the thigh
that was resting on top of hers, but it wasn't easy. In fact, it
was getting harder by the moment.

Clay cleared his throat. The thigh slipped lower and an
arm came around her waist and turned her toward him.

> ''When asked by sundry and all
> To be at their beck and their call
> Joelle couldn't wait
> To accommodate
> Their every need, large ones or small.''

''I'm still waiting,'' she prompted.

''I'm not finished,'' he declared.

> ''Then along came a man with a need
> That he desperately wanted to plead
> But Abbott was worried,
> His lofty brow furried—''

''Furried?'' scoffed Jo.

''All right, furrowed,'' Clay said. ''Now, be quiet and let
the bard complete his work. Where was I?''

''Something about a need?''

''It rhymes with plead,'' Clay said defensively.

''It's not going to work. You just don't have the courage, do you?''

Clay took a deep breath. Looking her directly in the eye,
he said slowly, ''I, Clayton Larkin Abbott, love thee, Joelle
Middleton. That's love, spelled L-O-V-E. A four letter word
meaning forever, and commitment, and all the rest of our

lives to share and explore together the riches of mind and body.''

Moved beyond words, Jo placed her lips on his. It was a slow, sweet kiss, one that offered everything and demanded nothing in return. By the time it ended, it was all she could do to speak. Clay held her as if he were afraid she might break, and unexpectedly, Jo began to laugh, her voice thick with emotion.

"That was beautiful, Clay. Browning couldn't have said it better."

"I think I can do the plainer version, too," he offered modestly. "I love you. I love—"

 # Silhouette Desire

COMING NEXT MONTH

BRIGHT RIVER—Doreen Owens Malek
Jessica's father had thought that Jack Chabrol had been an
unacceptable suitor for a daughter of Bright River's wealthiest family.
Could love temper Jack's bitterness when fate brought Jessica back?

BETTING MAN—Robin Elliott
Kate Jennings could make book on the fact that Griff Hayden was
perfect for her ad campaign. Griff was determined to convince her
that all bets were off when it came to love.

COME FLY WITH ME—Sherryl Woods
Who was that man following Lindsay Tabor around Los Angeles
Airport? However preoccupied Lindsay may have been, Mark
Channing wasn't a man she could easily ignore.

CHOCOLATE DREAMS—Marie Nicole
Keith Calloway was a man with a mission, and satisfying the world's
cocoa cravings was priority number one. But vivacious Terri McKay
quickly had this serious-minded man dreaming of forbidden treats.

GREAT EXPECTATIONS—Amanda Lee
Megan couldn't share her secret with anyone, least of all
Greg Alexander. Her project was too close to bearing fruit to blow
her cover—yet she knew Greg could deliver the dream of a lifetime.

SPELLBOUND—Joyce Thies
According to Denise Palmer, Ph.D., Taggart Bradshaw was a
stress-prone type A and therefore Mr. Wrong for her. So why was
Taggart bent on showing Denise just how right he could be?

AVAILABLE NOW:

ATTRACTIVE, SPACE SAVING BOOK RACK

Display your most prized novels on this handsome and sturdy book rack. The hand-rubbed walnut finish will blend into your library decor with quiet elegance, providing a practical organizer for your favorite hard-or soft-covered books.

Only $9.95

Approximately 16" x 8" when assembled

Assembles in seconds!

To order, rush your name, address and zip code, along with a check or money order for $10.70* ($9.95 plus 75¢ postage and handling) payable to *Silhouette Books*.

Silhouette Books
Book Rack Offer
901 Fuhrmann Blvd.
P.O. Box 1325
Buffalo, NY 14269-1325

Offer not available in Canada.

*New York residents add appropriate sales tax.

BKR-2R

Take 4 Silhouette Intimate Moments novels FREE

Then preview 4 brand new Silhouette Intimate Moments® novels —delivered to your door every month—for 15 days as soon as they are published. When you decide to keep them, you pay just $2.25 each ($2.50 each, in Canada), *with no shipping, handling, or other charges of any kind!*

Silhouette Intimate Moments novels are not for everyone. They were created to give you a more detailed, more exciting reading experience, filled with romantic fantasy, intense sensuality, and stirring passion.

The first 4 Silhouette Intimate Moments novels are absolutely FREE and without obligation, yours to keep. You can cancel at any time.

You'll also receive a FREE subscription to the Silhouette Books Newsletter as long as you remain a member. Each issue is filled with news on upcoming titles, interviews with your favorite authors, even their favorite recipes.

To get your 4 FREE books, fill out and mail the coupon today!

Silhouette Books, 120 Brighton Rd., P.O. Box 5084, Clifton, NJ 07015-5084

**Clip and mail to: Silhouette Books,
120 Brighton Road, P.O. Box 5084, Clifton, NJ 07015-5084***

YES. Please send me 4 FREE Silhouette Intimate Moments novels. Unless you hear from me after I receive them, send me 4 brand new Silhouette Intimate Moments novels to preview each month. I understand you will bill me just $2.25 each, a total of $9.00 (in Canada, $2.50 each, a total of $10.00)—with no shipping, handling, or other charges of any kind. There is no minimum number of books that I must buy, and I can cancel at any time. The first 4 books are mine to keep. *Silhouette Intimate Moments available in Canada through subscription only.*

BIM587

Name _____ (please print) _____

Address _____ Apt. # _____

City _____ State/Prov. _____ Zip/Postal Code _____

* In Canada, mail to: Silhouette Canadian Book Club,
320 Steelcase Rd., E., Markham, Ontario, L3R 2M1, Canada
Terms and prices subject to change.
SILHOUETTE INTIMATE MOMENTS is a service mark and registered trademark.

IM-SUB-1A

Take 4 Silhouette
Special Edition novels
FREE
and preview future books in your home for 15 days!

When you take advantage of this offer, you get 4 Silhouette Special Edition® novels FREE and without obligation. Then you'll also have the opportunity to preview 6 brand-new books —delivered right to your door for a FREE 15-day examination period—as soon as they are published.

When you decide to keep them, you pay just $1.95 each ($2.50 each in Canada) *with no shipping, handling, or other charges of any kind!*

Romance *is* alive, well and flourishing in the moving love stories of Silhouette Special Edition novels. They'll awaken your desires, enliven your senses, and leave you tingling all over with excitement...and the first 4 novels are yours to keep. You can cancel at any time.

As an added bonus, you'll also receive a FREE subscription to the Silhouette Books Newsletter as long as you remain a member. Each issue is filled with news on upcoming books, interviews with your favorite authors, even their favorite recipes.

To get your 4 FREE books, fill out and mail the coupon today!

Silhouette Special Edition®

Silhouette Books, 120 Brighton Rd., P.O. Box 5084, Clifton, NJ 07015-5084

Clip and mail to: Silhouette Books,
120 Brighton Road, P.O. Box 5084, Clifton, NJ 07015-5084 *

YES. Please send me 4 FREE Silhouette Special Edition novels. Unless you hear from me after I receive them, send me 6 new Silhouette Special Edition novels to preview each month. I understand you will bill me just $1.95 each, a total of $11.70 (in Canada, $2.50 each, a total of $15.00), with no shipping, handling, or other charges of any kind. There is no minimum number of books that I must buy, and I can cancel at any time. The first 4 books are mine to keep.

B1SS87

Name	(please print)	

Address		Apt. #

City	State/Prov.	Zip/Postal Code

* In Canada, mail to: Silhouette Canadian Book Club, 320 Steelcase Rd., E.,
Markham, Ontario, L3R 2M1, Canada
Terms and prices subject to change.   SE-SUB-1A
SILHOUETTE SPECIAL EDITION is a service mark and registered trademark.

Breathtaking adventure and romance
in the mystical land of the pharaohs...

YESTERDAY
~AND~
TOMORROW

ERIN YORKE

A young British archeologist, Cassandra Baratowa, embarks
on an adventurous romp through Egypt in search of Queen
Nefertiti's tomb—and discovers the love of her life!

———————————◆◆◆———————————

Available in MARCH, or reserve your copy for February shipping by sending your
name, address, zip or postal code along with a check or money order for $4.70 (in-
cludes 75¢ for postage and handling) payable to Worldwide Library to:

In the U.S.	In Canada
Worldwide Library	Worldwide Library
901 Fuhrmann Blvd.	P.O. Box 609
Box 1325	Fort Erie, Ontario
Buffalo, NY 14269-1325	L2A 9Z9

Please specify book title with your order.

⊕ WORLDWIDE LIBRARY   YES-1